Henry H. Vivian

Notes of a Tour in America

From August 7th to November 17th, 1877

Henry H. Vivian

Notes of a Tour in America
From August 7th to November 17th, 1877

ISBN/EAN: 9783337190996

Printed in Europe, USA, Canada, Australia, Japan

Cover: Foto ©Andreas Hilbeck / pixelio.de

More available books at **www.hansebooks.com**

NOTES OF A TOUR

IN AMERICA.

FROM AUGUST 7TH TO NOVEMBER 17TH, 1877.

BY

H. HUSSEY VIVIAN, M.P., F.G.S.

"Neque semper arcum tendit Apollo."—*Horace.*

LONDON:
EDWARD STANFORD, 55, CHARING CROSS.

1878.

SWANSEA :

PRINTED AT "THE CAMBRIAN" OFFICE,

WIND-STREET.

Dedication.

I DEDICATE THESE NOTES TO MY TRAVELLING COMPANIONS,

TO THE

RIGHT HON. HUGH C. E. CHILDERS, M.P.,

TO WHOSE KINDNESS I OWE THE INCEPTION,

TO WHOSE FORETHOUGHT I OWE THE SUCCESSFUL COMPLETION,

AND TO WHOSE INTELLIGENT COMPANIONSHIP I OWE SO MUCH OF THE

PLEASURE AND PROFIT OF MY TOUR;

TO

MISS CHILDERS,

WHOSE PRESENCE EVER CHEERED AND CHARMED OUR JOURNEYING,

AND TO

MY WIFE,

WHO, UNDER ALL CIRCUMSTANCES, AND EVERYWHERE, SHED A

BRIGHT BEAM OF SUNSHINE ON OUR PATH.

H. HUSSEY VIVIAN.

PREFACE.

———•———

" THE following Notes of a Tour in North America
will probably contain nothing new, and, it is to be
hoped, nothing in the nature of adventure. They
will pretend to no literary merit: they will be
written for their writer's amusement and future
reference. If the proprietor of THE CAMBRIAN
thinks they will interest his readers, they are much
at their and his service."

Such was the prophetic preface despatched from
Canada with the first of these Notes, and as I believe the prophesy has been realized in all particu-
lars, a few words only of explanation to the general
reader need be added as to how and why they had
any existence, and are now reprinted almost ver-
batim.

It has been my custom, when travelling, to jot

down what I saw, partly to fix it in my memory,
partly for reference. I began to write such private
notes after landing in Canada. It then occurred to
me that it might interest my neighbours at home to
know how the New World looked to an old friend,
and the Notes were slipped into an envelope ad-
dressed to "THE CAMBRIAN Newspaper," a steady,
well-conducted journal established at Swansea in
1804. On my return I found that the Notes
had been read with interest, not alone by my
neighbours, but by many at a distance, and I
was much pressed to republish them. My friends
probably take too partial a view, and thus over-
value the merit of this plain and homely tale of an
ordinary tour in a well-trodden land. However, the
kind appreciation of this slight effort which I have
received has already repaid any trouble tenfold, and
the race is therefore won before the start.

One more sentence: Any profit arising from the
sale of this little work will go in aid of the Building
Fund of St. John's Church, Swansea, a Parish without a church, but with nearly five thousand inhabitants, in whose welfare I am deeply interested. The
Proprietor of THE CAMBRIAN has liberally under-
taken to do the printing at cost price in furtherance
of the good work. Perhaps some of my kind

readers may also be moved to give us a helping hand. At any rate, if anyone buys my book and thinks he has paid too much, he may comfort himself by putting the "balance" down to charity. If anyone buys it and thinks it worth more than he paid for it he may quiet his conscience by remitting the balance to the Building Committee of St. John's Church, Swansea.

HENRY HUSSEY VIVIAN.

PARKWERN,
    15TH AUGUST, 1878.

CONTENTS.

NOTES

OF

A TOUR IN NORTH AMERICA.

CHAPTER I.

DEPARTURE.

EIGHTEEN hundred years ago or thereabout old
Horace, who was not cursed with penny postage or
shilling telegrams, wrote, " *Neque semper arcum
tendit Apollo.*" Our wise old saw changes Apollo
into Jack, and freely renders it that " All work and
no play makes Jack a dull boy."

Our instinct of self-preservation bids us obey these
old laws ; and as August approaches I hear, in the
particular portion of the House of Commons library
I usually inhabit in common with the maps, the click
of their reeds constantly sounding, and the whispered
schemes of worn-out M.P.'s for the Autumn holiday.

Mine were fixed before Easter at a quiet corner
table at the Athenæum ; " Have you ever been in

B

America ?" " No ; it is one of the unrealized dreams of my life." " My daughter and myself are going to make a tour there after the Session ; how charming if you and your wife will join us ; you will be well cared for, and all made easy ;" too tempting an offer to decline ; and so my Autumn holiday was arranged, and berths taken in the Allan liner, " Caspian," for the 7th August.

The time arrives in spite of the Obstructives, and we take leave of our bright home and lovely bay. Shall we see aught so bright and lovely in our long wanderings ? I doubt it ; for Europe has few such charming spots, and I expect none more beautiful in the New World.

The London and North-Western Railway lands us two hours late at Liverpool, which looks and smells as murky and grimy as during the three years I spent there thirty-three years ago, relieved by nothing but the great kindness of its inhabitants. The morning broke darkly, smoke and drizzle combining to keep up the character of its odious climate. After paddling about and making last purchases, we embarked in heavy rain and half a gale on board the tender, and thence scaled the sides of the " Caspian." Then came the effort to squeeze one's traps and oneself into one's " State-room," a cell 7 by 7 by 7½ feet.

The last goods hoisted on board, the tender leaves, and we steam down Channel, drop our pilot, and head for Queenstown. It looks dirty, the glass has fallen nearly 8-10ths, and I know it must blow ; but at present the water is smooth. We remain on deck

till darkness obscures the distant coasts of North
Wales; light after light, now revolving, now glowing
red over the turbid waters, opens and fades, and
then we try to turn in; but the mattress is some
inches narrower than our shoulders, and everything
seems to take wanton pleasure in hitting us on the
head. However, in spite of all discomforts, uncon-
sciousness supervenes, and except that our cell begins
to perform most eccentric antics, one might believe
oneself at rest.

The breakfast bell rings, and we attempt to dress.
Then, indeed, the full force of discomfort breaks upon
us. The breakfast looks uninviting, and we scramble
up the companion; but the sea looks wild and
dirty; through the mist we see the surf breaking
on the Tuska, the light-house just visible. It is
blowing a heavy gale, and everyone is "down," or
nearly so. Was it wise to leave one's bright and
happy home, with every comfort about one for such
"pleasure" as this? Hope alone can justify it.

Queenstown is reached; still blowing hard; but
the glass is rising, and the gale will soon be over.
Our last letters written; our last telegram flashed;
the tender leaves; the pilot is dropped, and then she
heads for the broad Atlantic.

Cape Clear light, called the "Fastenet," appears
and sinks over the taffrail. Our voyage is fairly and
irretrievably begun.

Soon our cell behaves better; it has to some extent
got over its state of intoxication, and stands up more
respectably, and, moreover, we become daily more

used to each other ; strange as it would at first have seemed, in the end we quite get to like each other.

Breakfast looks excellent and justifies its appearance ; ditto dinner and supper thenceforth. Day after day the frailer passengers, male and female, emerge. At last we are a united and happy family, and all goes merrily.

It is true that on Saturday, the 11th August, the glass fell 5-10ths, and a stiff breeze stiffened into half a gale in the night ; but by that time the passengers had got their sea brains, and bravely assembled at service on the Sunday morning.

Reading, pacing the fine flush deck, shuffle board, ring quoits, &c., caused the time to pass pleasantly enough. The "run" was eagerly watched as soon as it was posted each afternoon : Liverpool to Queenstown, 240 ; August 9, 181 ; August 10, 278 ; August 11, 295 ; August 12, 313 ; August 13, 300 ; August 14, 284 ; distant from St. John's, Newfoundland, 86 miles ; total, 1977. It was evident that at twelve knots per hour, we ought to make St. John's harbour at 7 p.m., and about 4.30 we all began to congregate forward and strain our eyes ahead. At last the captain declared that land was in sight, and there it was—a thin blue streak, an inch high, below the fleecy white clouds. We gazed for the first time on that New World, which has developed itself with such giant strides, and is destined to exert so powerful an influence on the near and far future. That man must indeed be possessed of a "dead soul" who could so gaze without emotion.

The land rose rapidly as we hung over the bows, and the vessel ploughed quickly through the calm blue sea, myriads of star and jelly-fish floating suspended like parachutes in the clear water. We soon made out the narrow entrance to St. John's, with its high cliffs, signal hill, and old battery. We were indeed heading exactly for it before we sighted land, so true had been our course, and at 7 p.m. we ran in through the narrow entrance, scarcely 100 yards wide, and opened out the fine capacious basin which forms the harbour, perfectly landlocked and sheltered from all winds.

Very soon we were alongside the quay, and once again on *terra firma*, just six days from Queenstown, and really a most agreeable six days they were. At this time of year, and in any of the first-class liners, an Atlantic voyage need have no terrors for the weakest nerves, and the only wonder is that in the intensely hackneyed and overcrowded condition of the usual "outings," more people do not "cross the ferry," as the Americans now call it, instead of jostling through the beaten tourist tracks of Europe.

The "Caspian" was scarcely alongside when an aide-de-camp from the Governor, Sir H. Glover, came on board with a hospitable invitation to Government House, where we were soon seated at a regular English dinner table. The garden was full of our English flowers, the temperature delicious, and we sat out after dinner in the fine warm night air, fragrant with the perfume of mignionette, roses, &c.,

in strong and grateful contrast to the cabin of the
" Caspian."

It is probable that some who may read this are
as ignorant of Newfoundland as I was before I visited
it, and I may therefore mention that it is an Island
about as large as Ireland ; possesses an independent
Legislature (not yet being part of the Dominion of
Canada) ; that its Parliament sits in all due form ;
and that a member is said to have once spoken for
18 hours. The Irish element is powerful among the
colonists ; the Scotch are also in force ; and England
has contributed her share. Religious feeling runs
high—Episcopalians, Nonconformists, and Roman
Catholics being nearly in equal proportions. The
education question has given as much trouble in
this remote spot as elsewhere, separate grants having
been forced on the Protestants, much to the deterioration of the schools, as was explained to me by an
intelligent Wesleyan Minister, a fellow-passenger
from England. There are only about 60,000 inhabitants in the whole island, and those are located
chiefly round the coast, and are engaged in the
fisheries. Most of the interior is in its primitive
condition, and some even unexplored and without
roads. Caraboo (the American reindeer), bears,
wolves, and smaller game, are abundant ; but it is
rough work to hunt them—impossible without
Indians, who are not easy to get.

The steamer was to leave at 9 a.m. We therefore
made an early start, and just as the day began to
dawn, at 5 a.m., were under weigh to see the town

and suburbs. We drove some miles to the westward, and making a circuit returned through the town, passing through the northern suburbs, and returning to our ship just as she was getting under weigh. The country gave me the idea of a highlying district, although little above the sea level, owing, I presume, to the length and severity of the winter. The vegetation was much what one sees at 2,000 feet above the sea : stunted trees and backward crops of oats and rye ; the hay not in, and coarse ; barley and wheat do not succeed ; turnips and potatoes excellent ; the forest trees are chiefly spruce, ash, birch, alder, poplar, elm—much the same as with us. Fishing, however, not agriculture, is the chief industry of Newfoundland. It is difficult to exaggerate the abundance of cod ; other fish, and even lobsters are despised, cod being the staple of the deep, and alone regarded as "fish," *par excellence,* by the New-foundlander.

On the whole, St. John's, Newfoundland, did not smile on me, and I was not sorry to be again on board and heading for more genial climes. Five hundred and thirteen miles to Halifax ! We run along the iron-bound coast of Newfoundland, sight and pass Cape Race, and shape our course across the Gulf of St. Lawrence direct for Halifax, where, barring fogs, we ought to be at 8 a.m. on Friday— about 48 hours' run. Thanks to a stiff breeze, the fog cleared, and at 5 a.m. on the second morning, I found we were rapidly running in towards land, glowing under a brilliant sunrise; the sea was studded with smart fishing schooners, their well-cut white cotton sails standing beautifully in the breeze, with smaller craft, more like our Swansea pilot boats than any craft I have ever seen elsewhere, filling up the scene. The grand harbour of Halifax was just opening as I got on deck. Its importance was soon manifest, for as we sped swiftly on, Batteries seemed to frown upon us from every point of vantage, and a small island in mid-channel, heavily armed, looked as if it could blow anything out of water.

Although the position of Halifax is most commanding when viewed from a distance, there is nothing of interest in the town itself. The main streets necessarily run along the steep hill side on which it is built, but they are in the last degree dirty and ill-kept; the pavements partly wooden and partly stone, are irregular, and frequently altogether absent, while the roads are deep in mud; the houses are ill-built, except the most recent; the place has, in fact, no attractions *per se*, but its surroundings are very charming. The outer harbour is magnificent—some five miles long by a mile broad; at its northern extremity it narrows to, say 100 yards, and then opens out into an inner harbour or sea Loch, called Bedford Basin, some ten miles long and two to three wide, its shores rising from 100 to 200 feet in beautifully wooded undulations, covered with natural forests. The drive along the shores of this basin is a constant pleasure to the inhabitants, shaded as it is by maple, common and hemlock spruce, pine, beech, and birch woods, while the fine expanse of Bedford Basin, with its clear blue waters, deep and broad enough for fleets to manœuvre in, form an ever changing contrast to the forest.   Crossing the narrow neck of land from the base of Bedford Basin to the south-west, we strike the head of another land-locked arm of Halifax Harbour, called the North-West Arm, along which the wealthier inhabitants have built their villas. Their gay gardens and grounds stretch down to the sea, and their boat-houses, bathing-houses, &c., give evidence of happy home life.

Perhaps the most striking feature of Halifax is its citadel, which crowns the hill, along the face of which the town is built, and with its well-kept glacis and 18-ton guns, seems capable of giving a good account of any invaders.   But, alas, I fear much good money must yet be spent before Halifax becomes what it ought to be—"impregnable."   It is now the only fortified position held by Great Britain in North America, and it may be said to command the most important portion of the seaboard, if in the hands of a Power possessing a strong Navy.   As a naval station, with an extensive coalfield at its back, it is of the last importance to England, and the necessary means should be found to place its defences in a more satisfactory condition than I found them, after closer investigation, to be in.

A very pleasant trip to every portion of the harbour in a steam launch brought our stay at Halifax to an end, and we made our way to the station of the Intercolonial Railway, which has been recently constructed by the Dominion, assisted by our Government, in order to open up the resources of Nova Scotia and New Brunswick, and to give the Dominion a winter harbour for its produce. In this respect also Halifax is now doubly important, and should be made secure. The Intercolonial Railway intersects both Nova Scotia and New Brunswick, passsing the Pictou Coalfield, which it opens both to Halifax and Upper Canada. It traverses a wild and sparsely settled country, and is not expected to pay, but it must exercise a most important influence on the provinces through which it passes, as well as on the whole Dominion.

On reaching the station, we found our " Pullman," or rather " Wagner" car, awaiting us, and perhaps a short description of it may not be uninteresting to those who are unacquainted with such conveyances. Imagine a very minute church with nave and lean-to aisles (without pillars) on wheels, and you have a fair section of an American Pullman Car. Close to the aisle windows are the pews or seats, and a passage passes down the centre; the seats are *meant* to hold two in width, and face each other ; at night they slide down, meet, and make a capital bed, far better than any berth on board ship, in fact all a traveller could desire. Our car conductor tells me that at the time of the " Centennial" they used to have a queer lot of " outwesters," and that as many as six have slept in one of these beds. Upon my expressing my incredulity, he explained that they consisted of " an old man and his wife and four

children." He declared that three were quite " com-
monly" packed into one at that crowded time—two
one way and one the other. It might be possible,
but not pleasant.

So much for the lower berth. The upper one,
representing the slanting roof of the aisle, lets
down with a hinge, and forms an excellent berth,
quite as large as the lower one ; the roof above
it now appears domed or curved outwards, and
in this dome the bedding, mattresses, &c., are
stowed during the day ; the under portion of the
upper berth is finely panelled mahogany, inlaid and
ornamented, and when closed up, could not be sus-
pected of forming a bed ; the beds, being arranged,
fill the width of the aisle ; the nave remains, forming
the passage from end to end of the car, with clear story
windows and lofty roof. At the junction of the aisle
and nave roofs runs a strong bar, upon which heavy
curtains are hooked, which form a complete screen,
while ample means of ventilation exist above the bar.
Between each two berths, or "section" as it is called, a
strong mahogany panel is bolted, forming as effectual
a separation as a bulkhead on board ship.

Having now passed five nights in these cars, I
can safely say that I much prefer them to many
sleeping quarters it has been my lot to occupy. At
each end of the car there are excellent lavatory
arrangements. Our car has also a separate bed-
room for ladies. Some have drawing-rooms,
cooking stoves, &c. Untold sums are squan-
dered on some of these cars, but an average

Pullman costs 15,000 dols., or £3,000. For the immense distances traversed on this Continent they are indispensable; but for England generally, I think our system is preferable. A Pullman weighs from 20 to 30 tons, or about one ton of dead weight to each passenger carried,—a fearful waste of locomotive power. They fit in well with the American central passage system, but not with our side-door carriages. I have been thus particular in describing the " Pullman car," because they form an essential portion of the railway life of America, and much of my time will be passed both night and day in them.

Night closed in upon a wild unsettled, *i.e.*, uninhabited country. Low hills covered with natural forest, chains of lakes following close upon each other, here and there a clearing but mostly wearying forest; the trees not fine, but apparently stunted before they came to maturity; the ground is rocky and I fancy not deep enough for fine trees. The scene reminded me most vividly of Sweden, with its never ending lakes and forests. Night passed away, and I woke with the dawn, to find we were running through much the same country; but in the night we had passed the Nova Scotian coal field, which I much regretted not to have seen. There was no day train which I could have taken. I hear there are five pits at work, but none of them are making much money—neighbours' fare. The coal I saw is hard and bituminous, but the account the Allan line officers gave of it was anything but satisfactory. I believe, however, that their owners did not hit upon the best when they acquired

their colliery, as I have an account before me of good
duty done by Nova Scotian coal.   The veins are
thick ; I am told that one is 40 feet thick, and others
18 and 20 feet, but such thicknesses do not mean
easy and cheap working.   The area of the coal fields
in this neighbourhood were stated before the Royal
Coal Commission to be 1,950 square miles, while
those of Great Britain are about 2,900 square miles,
so that the coal of the Dominion of Canada may play
a very important part in its future history, especially
as they are on or close to its seaboard.

Being like John Gilpin " on pleasure bent," I did
not devote a day to a superficial survey of this coalfield.   My hopes lay in a few casts on an American
salmon river, the electric shock of a good fish's first
dash, a " tight line," and gallant fight; so we pushed
on for the Nipisiquit river, which falls into the Bay
of Chaleurs, at a place called Bathurst.   Whatever
may be the temperature for six months in the year,
and it is Arctic, at this time we are able to appreciate
the fitness of the name given to this magnificent
Bay, " Chaleur," by its discover Jacques Cartier, in
July, 1534, for the heat is intense, 80 deg. to 85 deg.
in the shade, and not a breath of wind.

We whipped the Nipisiquit in vain, barring a few
5lb. grilse ; in fact, it is too late for large salmon,
which have all run up to the upper waters.   In June
they say the fishing in these New Brunswick rivers
of the Bay of Chaleurs, the Restigouche, Metapadiac,
Nipisiquit, &c., is wonderful, but like Norway it is
inconsistent with Parliamentary life.   We, however,

made the attempt. A drive of three miles from the neat little settlement of Bathurst brought us to the "rough waters," where for a mile or more the Nipisiquit foams over rapids, formed by granite rocks stretching across its course. We found a colony of fishermen located close by, for the most part the descendants of old French settlers, and still, among themselves, talking their old language, but at the same time speaking English without an accent. There were Bouchers, Vinos, &c.; among others Joe Young, who spoke with an unmistakably broad Cornish accent and looked the Cornishman all over, though speaking half his time in French. He declared he was not Cornish; but on my asking him where his forefathers came from he said "from Cornwall," but the word Cornish was unknown to him; his "grand grand father" had been captain of a vessel, and had settled there 15 years before Wolfe took Quebec. The old blood and tongue had come down through three generations, and he was as typical a Cornishman as any from the Landsend to the Tamar.

These men are expert in managing the Indian birch bark canoe, a delightful craft; they poled it up impracticable rapids even with my weight in it, and guided it with paddles through broken dashing falls, where one would not believe so frail a thing could live; when the falls are too high they "portage" the canoe as fast as one can follow them.

As we were fishing among the broken waters two Mic-mac Indians floated gravely past in their canoe with all their worldly goods, moving camp, their squaws meeting them below the "rough waters." There was something very spectral in their silent solemn gliding by, and it made one realize that one was not in the old country. These Mic-mac Indians are scattered over Nova Scotia and New Brunswick. Near Halifax we came upon one of their settlements, and here and there we saw them along the railroad. They are an ugly coarse broad featured race, without much to recommend them. I prefer the Niggers, whom we saw in considerable numbers in the neighbourhood of Dartmouth opposite Halifax, to which place they had come with their farm produce to market. We passed as many carts full of them grinning, chattering, and full of fun as you would pass on the Gower-road of a Saturday night. They are I believe in part the descendants of slaves captured by our cruisers, and in part of runaway slaves from the States.

After spending two very pleasant but very hot days on the Nipisiquit our car was hooked on to the express at 6 a.m., and we were again whirling away through forest and clearing in a due north line for the St. Lawrence. Our route lay along the south side of the beautiful Bay of Chaleurs: a fine range of mountains bounds it on the north, covered with forest, and rising from 2,000 to 3,000 feet, reminding me much of the Riviera, without however the high tops of the Maritime Alps beyond. The cloudless sky and deep blue waters were quite Italian ; indeed our latitude is about the same as the Riviera, although we are too apt to think of Canada as Arctic rather than Italian. At the head of the Bay of Chaleur, the Restigouche debouches, and within a short distance is the month of the Metapidiac, up the narrow gorge of which the Intercolonial is carried for 50 or 60 miles, till it reaches the Lake of the same name. The gorge of the Metapidiac is a very fine bold bit of mountain scenery; hills probably attaining 2,000 feet in height, terminating in sharp outlines and peaks, rise almost from the margin of the clear waters of the river and virgin forests, which have thus far escaped the Lumberer's axe, cling to the steep sides and climb to the mountain tops. From the Lake of Metapediac to the northern watershed is but a short run, and we then descend on the gulf of St. Lawrence, and run along its southern shores to the Station opposite Quebec.

At first the gulf is too wide to allow the opposite shore to be seen, but mile by mile it narrows till at Quebec we reach the mighty St. Lawrence River, representing the water-shed of a million square miles, the offspring of the greatest chain of lakes of the American Continent—Lakes Superior, Michigan, Huron, Erie, and Ontario. The eye cannot measure and guage these mighty rivers. Opposite Quebec the St. Lawrence must be from a mile to a mile and a half wide, with depth enough for large ships, over its entire width. The English Fleet of ironclads was at anchor on its deep and ample bosom far beyond the tidal influence, and dwarfed into almost insignificance by the grandeur of the scenery around them.

CHAPTER II.

QUEBEC.

QUEBEC is certainly a most striking city and full
of interest; it stands on a bold promontory at the
confluence of the small river St. Charles with the St.
Lawrence. Towards the latter, the rock rises in a
sheer precipice, about 500 feet, and is surmounted by
the fine old Citadel, associated with so many ever
memorable events in our history. The citadel closely
resembles Ehrenbreitstein, the great German fortress
opposite Coblentz on the Rhine. All but externally,
however, the glory of Quebec has departed; it no
longer embodies the might of Great Britain; its streets
no longer echo to the step of armed legions; the British
ensign has been formally "hauled down"; the British
troops are withdrawn, the small but gallant staff
of the Canadian Artillery Militia are now its sole
occupants.

Since the withdrawal of the British troops the
city has sunk into greater dullness than ever; its
want of active commerce was conspicuous even to us
casual travellers. It is, in fact, an old French town,
with its traditions and reliques, quaint old houses,
and steep narrow streets, dating from its foundation
in 1608, from which period till Wolfe's great victory
in 1759 it remained in the possession of the French.

D

The view in every direction from the citadel is most magnificent, commanding, as it does, a panorama of the whole surrounding country and the reaches of the St. Lawrence for many miles. To the north-west are the plains of Abraham, running up to the citadel, where the gallant Wolfe and Montcalm, though both wounded early in the battle, fought out the live long day, and closed it only with their deaths,—the one at the moment of victory, the other at the moment of defeat. What Englishman can contemplate that battle-field without feelings of emotion ? To me it was indeed interesting, for there my great great uncle, Colonel Hussey, fell at the head of his regiment—the last of his race.

The chief incidents of the battle were well explained to us by Colonel Strange, R.A., Inspector of Canadian Artillery Militia, who kindly accompanied us over the field, now desecrated by a huge prison, villas, and the like, which have changed its face and swept away the ancient landmarks, but the leading features and glorious association must ever remain.

Before leaving Quebec we drove to the Falls of Montmorency, some eight miles below the city, on the north bank of the St. Lawrence. Our route lay through an almost continuous street of small detached houses and holdings, owned by the descendants of the French settlers. On the other side of the river, in approaching Quebec, we had passed through 200 miles of similarly inhabited country, the chief seat of the old French colonists. The French law, as to the division of property, has prevailed through many generations, and the result is that the holdings have become smaller and smaller by constant division. Frontage to the main road being all important, the divisions have been made by separating the holdings, from the road backwards, so that they have now become almost the mathematical definition of straight lines, narrow frontage, and great depth. Many of the holdings seem to be 20 or 30 yards wide, and a mile or more deep, most expensive and inconvenient for cultivation.

If anyone wishes to study the law of the compulsory division of property upon each death, they will be able to do so here to perfection ; and, by contrasting the condition of the English, Scotch, and Irish settlers with that of the French, they will soon, I think, be convinced that such a law is not calculated to advance the real interests of any community. There can be no doubt that if the younger children of these colonists had received sums of money, or cattle and sheep, to enable them to occupy fresh holdings, and to win fresh land from the forest, both they and the community would have reaped the benefit, just as our younger sons constitute the vigorous life of our race, and whether in the law court or the battle-field, in busy commerce or distant colonization, win their way to fortune, and advance their country's greatness. The life of a young Frenchman, heir to a few acres, is widely different, devoted, as it too often is, to the dissipations of town life.

The districts around Quebec are almost exclusively

of French settlement. Substantial churches were built by their first settlers, and remain to this day the chief places of worship, the French population continuing Roman Catholic. They are under the strict control of their priests, and are orderly and loyal to the British Crown. Their instincts are monarchical, and they know full well that under no other form of government would they enjoy such complete religious liberty, combined with the traditional connection of King and Priest so dear to the latter. In Quebec itself the English and French languages are spoken, and used in notices, &c., indiscriminately.

But I have forgotten the Falls of Montmorency, and I have not much to say about them, for I have seen many better worth an eight-mile drive. A river, perhaps as large as the Tawe, falls over a nearly precipitous cliff about 250 feet high. The Falls are pretty, but not grand.

In the afternoon we steamed away from Quebec, passing the Heights of Abraham, on our way to Montreal, by the St. Lawrence. As we glided by in the fast steamer, the outlines illuminated by the setting sun, we said to ourselves—" It was in that creek Wolfe landed his army in the dead of night, and there is the small wooded ravine up which they silently crept, till they gained the heights."

We breasted the current of the St. Lawrence at the rate of nearly 20 miles per hour, in one of the floating castles in which Americans delight. These river steamers are unique, and deserve a passing

word. Their hulls are just like ordinary river boats,
long, with a flat floor, fine entry, and plenty of
beam ; but upon this are built tiers of decks, surrounded with galleries far overhanging the ship's
sides. On the first deck are the baggage rooms, bar
(a most important American institution), second and
third-class, and sometimes first-class dining saloons,
cooking places, engines, &c. On the second deck is
a saloon running along the whole length of the ship,
perhaps 300 feet long, carpeted, and furnished with
ottomans, arm-chairs, tables, and every luxury of a
drawing-room, while along the sides are large and
most comfortable staterooms and bedrooms. The
third deck is also devoted to sleeping berths, with
external galleries. These steamers are propelled by
old-fashioned long-stroke beam engines, and paddles
of immense diameter.

There is little of interest on the St. Lawrence between Quebec and Montreal, and people desirous of
going from one to the other find it more convenient
to do the 180 miles by night in these fine steamers,
on board which they are as comfortable as in an hotel.
They are therefore the most popular mode of conveyance. We embarked in the evening, and found ourselves at Montreal without the least fatigue next
morning.

Montreal is the most important city in the
Dominion, as well as its commercial centre. It has
a population of about 110,000, but its rate of increase
is and has been very rapid. Ships of large burden
can now ascend the St. Lawrence to Montreal, in-

cluding Transatlantic steamers. The " lumber" (*i.e.*
timber) and grain trades are the staple trades of Montreal, and are actively pushed. It has all the appearance of one of our northern commercial towns,—broad
streets, and fine solid carved stone buildings, both public and private, religious, scientific, and commercial ;
but it has no special interest for the casual visitor.

It occupies a comparatively flat strip of land,
perhaps a mile wide, at the base of a remarkable
mountain, which protrudes through the alluvium,
and rears its almost perpendicular face 700 feet above
the town. From thence comes its name of the
" Royal Mount," given to it in honour of his master,
by Jacques Cartier, who discovered it in 1535. The
site of this now fine town was then occupied by an
Indian village. It was not until 100 years later that
it was settled by the French, after which it was
frequently attacked by the Indians. Montreal fell
into English hands in 1759, when its population
was only 4000.

The mob of Montreal is the worst in the Dominion, as was recently shown in the Orange riots.
Religious sects are pretty equally divided. There
is a new Episcopal Cathedral, designed by Scott,
which cost £60,000 ; an immense Jesuit Church
and College, as well as the fine Roman Catholic
Parish Church of Notre Dame, and a group of
handsome Nonconformist churches of various denominations, huddled close together. The feature
of the place, however, is the mountain, which is
beautifully wooded, and has been converted into a

park. Well-engineered roads are carried round it, gradually ascending to the summit, from which the views are magnificent. The town lies spread out for several miles along the banks of the St. Lawrence, and being largely built of red brick, glows in the glorious sunshine which now prevails; for it must be borne in mind that the latitude of Montreal is that of Venice, and, consequently, that the sun in summer has equal power; that the skies are as blue and the atmosphere as clear as that of Northern Italy. Ever since we landed at Halifax the heat has been really overpowering, ranging from 80 to 90 deg. in the shade, but the climate is nevertheless exhilarating and enjoyable after one becomes a little used to it. The cold in winter is excessive, owing no doubt to the north and north-west winds, which, I am told, prevail, and also to the absence of that great hot water apparatus, the Gulf Stream, which so completely modifies our climate.

Montreal is the commercial, but Ottawa is the political, capital of the Dominion, and, being only one day from Montreal, we resolved to visit it. The journey may be performed entirely by rail, or partly by rail and partly by steamer up the Ottawa river. We chose the latter, as we heard much of the beauties of the scenery. Starting by an early train from Montreal, after a short run we found the steamer waiting for us above the rapids of the St. Lawrence. After half-an-hour's steam up the great river, we remarked a line of discoloured water on its northern side, and soon found ourselves entering the mouth of

the Ottawa, which, from not passing through the
decanting process of the Lakes, bears down with it
its full charge of mud gathered in its course of 500
miles.   After steaming up the Ottawa for an hour
or two, we again had to take the train in order to
avoid the Rapids—the "portage" of early days.   A
short run by rail, and then an embarkation for a final
steam across the small Lake of "The Two Mountains,"
and up the river to Ottawa.

I confess I was not impressed by the scenery;
wooded islands and distant but not lofty or rugged
hills, make up its complement.   Pretty enough, but
not impressive.   The river itself is large, larger probably than any three of our English rivers combined,
but it is generally shallow and devoid of attractive
features.   It drains an extensive area, being nearly 500
miles in length, intersecting vast districts where the
lumberer's axe has never been heard, and bearing
annually a vast burthen of the primeval giants of the
forest down on its ample bosom to be dismembered
by the mighty power produced by its own waters,
where they boil and dash over a precipice forming
the beautiful "Chandiere," or "Cauldron" Falls, close
to the town of Ottawa.   A hundred ruthless tools,
from the frame and circular saw to the minute
"plough and tongue," or still more minute match-
making machines (what would some of our mammas
give for such a machine!) are set in motion by its
abundant waters, and yet the grandeur of the Falls
is in no way diminished.   Doors, windows, and
every other "lumber fixing," down to matches from

the slabs and refuse, are in fact now made at the
head-quarters, and in presence of the primeval forest,
not framed and fashioned by man's hand, but by
cunningly devised tools, set in motion by the costless
drainage of a wilderness. Let our craftsmen in wood
be warned, and beware how they pit their measured
hours against these simple but mighty combinations
of nature and art. I believe that no joinerwork, of
or belonging to a house, exists which could not be
ordered and sent from Ottawa, and many other places
in Canada, ready fitted and numbered for its place,
almost untouched by man's hand. It is hardly an
exaggeration to say that the log floats in at one end
of the establishment and leaves it in the form of
doors, windows, boards, roof parts, joists, and the
like, at the other end, without the sweat of man's
brow having fallen on it, all force having been supplied by the simple gravitation of falling water. The
incidence of freight and charges is also on the net and
not on the gross weight, nor does the stuff need to
pay toll to a dozen intermediaries.

But I have run ahead of my day's march. We
steamed up the Ottawa River between pleasantly
wooded banks, and past numerous islets until at
last the new-born Capital came in sight, crowning
a bluff on its southern shore.

The position of the Legislative Buildings is most
happily chosen. For some distance below Ottawa
a plateau, ending in a steep escarpment, is seen on
the right or southern shore, and parallel with it. This
escarpment suddenly bends to the north, cuts the

E

River at right angles, and forms the heights on which the City is built. The River leaping over the precipitous face of this escarpment, gives rise to the beautiful Chandiere Fall. The view from the terrace outside the building is very striking, and reminded me of the views from Windsor Castle, minus, however, the "distant spires and antique towers" of dear old Eton.

The Legislative Buildings are handsome and really creditable to the public spirit of the community : they are indeed a block of buildings not unworthy of any country. I am told that £600,000 has been expended on them. Their style is somewhat complex, but perhaps I shall not err in describing it as "rénaissance Gothic." The two Chambers are well adapted to their ends. Each member has his desk, and may write his letters or whatever he pleases during debates—this shocks my feelings ; but custom is everything, and it may be the young ones are right.

All the Government offices are under one roof with the Chambers, which must be a convenient arrangement; the Supreme Court is also within the area of the building. The Library demands special notice. It is a richly ornamented circular structure about 150 feet in diameter, with a lofty dome ; galleries run round it, and at eight points transverse galleries project from the main galleries, thus affording a greatly increased space for books. The Legislature was unfortunately not in Session when we visited Ottawa.

A railroad journey of seven hours brought us again to Montreal, from whence we embarked in our Pullman at 3.30 p.m., and at 8.30 next morning found ourselves at Boston, as fresh as if we had slept the sleep of four-posters. So long as daylight lasted we were passing through a fairly-cultivated country, much forest still standing, and many stumps appearing in the cultivated fields. Even as we approached Boston I was surprised to see such a large proportion of country still in its primitive condition; but it was rough stony land, and I called to mind Cobham, Ascot Heath, Woking, and the Surrey Downs, within a few miles of London, and wondered no longer.

Boston! How many historical recollections that name calls up! The first outbreaks of that rebellion which created a self-governing nation of Anglo-Saxons already as powerful as any nation in the old world, and probably destined far to exceed all other nations, took their rise here. The old church which was the resort of the conspirators, and was afterwards used as a stable by the British troops, is still standing. The spot is shown where the tea was thrown into the harbour to escape a duty which would now be thought light; the church tower from a window of which Revere and his wife showed the signal light to let their countrymen known that the British soldiers were crossing the creek; Bunker's Hill, a low hillock now built round in all directions, and surmounted by a fine granite obelisk. All these call up recollections politically painful to an Englishman, although the gallant deeds of Howe and Clinton on that 17th of June, 1775, must ever be remembered with pride by us. Why the Americans have erected that obelisk to commemorate their defeat I know not ! ! Our troops took their entrenched work, captured five out of six guns, and drove them out of their positions with a loss of 450 killed and wounded. It is true they fought gallantly, and inflicted on us a loss of somewhat more than double that number, which however only proves the bravery of our troops in attacking and carrying their entrenched positions. We can also look with pride at the entrance of Boston harbour, close to which that gallant deed of arms was done, when two evenly-matched frigates, the Chesapeake and Shannon, closed deliberately in their deadly strife ; and then, when an old pilot (not long dead) saw the thick smoke which hid them clear away, a sight was revealed which he declared haunted him nightly for long years after, for he saw the British ensign floating proudly over the stars and stripes. Boston involuntarily recalls these recollections of painful events brought about by the blind illiberality of a dark political age, and which, if possible, should be now forgotten.

The Bostonians are proud of their resemblance to the Old Country, and, in truth, their "city" (all places over 5,000 or so are "cities" here) bears much resemblance to an old English town, with its irregular narrow streets and substantial red brick houses, with bow windows. The test of respectability and the object of ambition in Boston is the possession of "a brown stone swell front," and when a man has attained to that he is what they call "at the top of the heap."

They are very proud also of their literary and scientific position, and boast that "their city is the 'Hub' of the Universe" (a "hub" is the nave of a wheel). A young Bostonian thus described their position to me :—"The Americans think we are an old and slow-going set, and we have certainly lost our influence entirely. When you are 'out West' you will see that not one paper devotes ten lines to Boston, while New York is quoted for everything ; but we turn out the men of high education, and are pre-eminent in all that concerns science and litera-ture." Harvard College is situated at Cambridge, in the environs of Boston.

The fashionable part of Boston adjoins the Park (called the "Common"), much as Piccadilly and Belgravia adjoin St. James's and the Green Park— indeed the lie of the ground is remarkably similar. The "Common" is a well kept and most ornamental space with fine trees, grass plots, flower beds, a small lake, and the other usual adjuncts of pleasure grounds ; it forms a healthy lung for this City, which now numbers some 350,000 inhabitants.

The commercial portion of Boston of course adjoins the harbour. We took good stock of the latter, having been shown every part of it by the resi-dent manager of the Cunard Company, who kindly placed at our disposal a fine screw tug. The harbour is of great extent,—I suppose ten miles

square,—shut in from the sea by promontories, reefs
and shoals: it is studded with islands, and surrounded with towns and villages.   The chief public
establishments, prisons, poor-houses, and the like,
are built upon the islands, but many of the latter are
still unoccupied.

In the course of our steam we were shown a remarkably useful buoy, off the mouth of the harbour,
which blows a whistle, automatically, as it rises and
falls in the seaway.   The sound is as loud as that of
a steam whistle (or hooter), and the captain of the
tug assured me he had heard it ten miles off.

The entrance to the harbour is tortuous, and the
forts on several of the islands look as if they could
give a good account of any intruder.   The dockyard
is deserted; no admiral-superintendent, and expensive staff of subs; no masses of shipwrights,
riggers, engineers, blockmakers, biscuit bakers, and
the like; no gigantic new basins and works in
construction; one sentry and a watchman or sleepy
guard or two were all we saw.   The United States
are paying off their Debt!!!

Fashionable Boston was "out of town," away at
Newport and Saratoga, the two great rival watering
places of North America, the one on the coast between
Boston and New York, the other 250 miles north,
far inland, and owing its origin to its mineral waters.
Time will not permit us to visit both these resorts
of pleasure seekers, so we once more embark in our
Pullman for "Saratoga," and turn our backs on
Newport.

" All aboard" is the American guard's warning,
and without waiting for "wicked man" or anyone
else, off the train goes, and woe betide the unready.

Our route lay by Worcester and Springfield to
Albany, thence by Troy to Saratoga. The country
between Boston and Albany may be described as a
hilly wooded district, with scarcely any flat agricultural land, except in the valley of Connecticut, which
we crossed at right angles; patches of cultivation,
patches of wood, rough stony hummocks, or " knows,"
as the Scotch call them, rather than hills, nothing high
or serrated; now we ran up a rocky valley, with its
clear stream and wooded banks, now we wound
through a hilly upland region, until at length we
descend upon the fertile and magnificent Hudson,
as broad as the Thames at Greenwich, and navigable
as far as Albany, by the floating castles I have before
described; in fact, the stream from New York to
Albany is, I am told, one of the most lovely things
on this Continent. After a short run from Albany,
we reached Saratoga, one of the Vanity Fairs of
America, which merits more than a passing notice
as illustrating one phase of the social life of our
Transatlantic brethren.

CHAPTER III.

SARATOGA.

To English ears the name of Saratoga has no association, causes no pulse to beat quicker. Far different is it with the young Americans of the northern cities. To them the name is associated with an annual outing, a month or six weeks of pleasure seeking. It forms one of the mile-stones of their year, to look forward to or look back at with joy or sorrow as the case may be.

The routine of the wealthy New Yorker was described to me to be much as follows :—October to Lent, the New York season, the gayest portion from December on—thence to May, quiet New York life. June, July, country and country-house life on the banks of the Hudson and other summer resorts. August, Saratoga. September, Newport, the great seaside resort, the Brighton of Tyburnia, the Cowes and Ryde of Belgravia, the Scarborough of Yorkshire.

Saratoga has risen from very small beginnings to its present greatness as a watering-place within a quarter of a century. Its hotels are on the largest scale I have ever seen. The " United States Hotel," at which we stayed, accommodates twelve hundred people. It has a total frontage of 445 of my paces, certainly upwards of 1,200 feet, and for most of its length, is five stories high. It is built round a quadrangle, the court being laid out as a parterre with grass plots, flower beds, fountains, and at one end, trees, &c. Around the sides, facing inwards, run lofty and wide arcades with boarded floors, upon which the occupants of the various suites of apartments, each of which is called a cottage, loll in their rocking chairs or pace to and fro. In the evening a fine band, which costs the proprietors £120 a week, plays in the quadrangle, except when there is a printed notice, as there was on the night of our arrival—" The band will not play to-night; a *hop* in the ball-room." We went to the hop and found an immense room well filled. The prevailing dance was the " Boston," a valse in very slow time, two steps forward, then one backwards by the gentleman, then two steps the wrong way round, and so on, *ad in-finitum.* They dance it with much ease and grace.

The hours of Saratoga are not late, nor early either ; breakfast 8 to 9, dinner 1 to 2, supper 6 to 7. Our friends had friends at Saratoga, who received us with all the cordiality and kindness imaginable, and we were soon quite at home in the gay world, and being posted up in the smartest Yankeyisms by the " brightest eyes in Saratoga."

The dangers of Saratoga may be estimated from the fact that there were no less than 47 widows in our hotel, many of them rich and charming, with every adjunct that Worth or La Ferriere, Elise or Mrs. Stratton, could supply. If the immortal Sam

F

Weller had been about to visit America, his anxious parent would have certainly barred Saratoga.

Drives to the 14 springs, each one more nauseous than the last; the Geyser, which squirts a stream the size of a pencil about ten feet into the air; the "Champion," a three inch column, 30 or 40 feet high, and so forth, constitute one of the chief attractions; but few visit Saratoga for the waters, pure and nasty, I fancy. Some no doubt do, and it is said that all manner of diseases are cured, but especially rheumatic affections.

Drives to St. George's Lake, boating and picnicking, races and trotting matches, make up the daily life of Saratoga. Trotting is the peculiar fancy of Americans. It is related that when the late Mr. or Commodore Vanderbilt (who died a few months ago worth 80,000,000 dollars, £16,000,000 sterling), married his last wife at the age of 78, and wished to give her such a treat as no other lady in America could enjoy, he trotted her out to the race course at Saratoga and round the "track" (*i.e.,* the mile) in 2 minutes 14 seconds, 2.20 being almost unparalleled.

But Saratoga is often the meeting place of great men, just as Gastein or Kissingen are the trysts of Emperors. The railway kings of America meet here, part in pleasure, part in earnest. The wires are often woven here for many a political combination. Even now I see the free traders of America have met at Saratoga and adopted strong resolutions against the present policy of protection.

While at Saratoga we were present at a telephone concert, startling and almost unearthly even in this age of wonders. The songs were sung at New York, and we heard them almost as clearly and distinctly at Saratoga as if but, a few feet instead of 250 miles separated us from the singers. Every note rang through the large room, and was heard by the 300 or 400 people present :—this is one of the most recent wonders of telegraphy, that marvellous, yet infant science. No one must be misled by the belief that the sound itself travels ; each wave of sound at New York sent its equivalent wave of electricity to Saratoga, which the sounding board, attached to the receiving apparatus, reconverted into a sound wave in the latter place,—this was the sound which we heard, not the actual voice of the singer. Talking was attempted ; the sound came, but I could not translate it ; the inflections of the human voice in speaking are too delicate for separate transmission at such a distance, although I am told that at five miles conversations can be carried on, and my friends at Hamilton, where I am now writing, have one in use between their office and the railway station, about 300 yards distant.

Our pleasant days at Saratoga came to an end, and we bid our kind friends adieu, to meet, we hope, later on at New York. Again we are aboard our Pullman, covering space insensibly while enjoying a good night's rest. Early dawn found us running through a rich and well-farmed country in the neighbour-hood of Rochester, on the southern shore of Lake

Ontario, along which the line passes to the Suspension Bridge over the gorge of Niagara, which we soon crossed, the steaming vapours of the great Fall rising high into the air on our left, and the vexed waters tearing through the narrow channel beneath us with terrific speed.

It was too late in the day when we arrived to do justice to this grand display of one of Nature's mightiest forces, and we pursued our journey to Hamilton at the western end of Ontario—an hour or so from Niagara—the head-quarters of the Great Western Railway of Canada, and therefore of ourselves.

He must be either more or less than human who could resist the impulse thoroughly to exhaust the varying phases of this most wonderful Fall, and we lost no time in devoting a long day to it. Some have expressed disappointment after first visiting Niagara. I cannot share their feelings. It impressed me with a sense of its own grandeur, and of the impotence of man, more than anything I ever yet saw, more than the Eruption of Vesuvius, the crashing of a Continental thunder-storm, or an ocean gale.

To convey an impression in the least degree adequate appears to me impossible. If to be viewed in a material sense, let the Engineer take his formula and calculate the equivalent of two million tons of water per minute, say 35,000 tons per second, falling from a height of 160 feet; and then let him say how many miles of locomotives, or how many first class ocean steam engines, or how many tons of "Ocean" steam coal the material force of Niagara represents. On my return home I found that the same idea had occurred to Dr. Siemens, and that he had calculated that if the whole of the coal produced from all the mines of the world were used for raising steam and applied in the most economical manner, it would not exert a force equal to the Falls of Niagara. Or, to view it from an æsthetic point, imagine a sea of raging waters, perhaps a mile and a half wide, dashing over ledges of rock, foaming, tossing its billows high into the air—on which no living thing floats, on which no living thing has ever floated and lived—rushing madly down a steep incline, suddenly contracted by the curving western shore into perhaps one third of its former width, and then leaping with one tremendous bound over a precipice of 160 feet; where shallow, broken at once into foam, but where deep (for perhaps 150 yards in width in the centre of the Fall) holding together in one green mass, for some sixty feet, and then separating into a seething veil of purest white, the whole volume dashing on to the rocky beach below, its contact lost in thickest vapours, then emerging, churned into snow-white foam which circles round and round for ever and for ever beneath the cataract, deafening with its roar, drenching all around with its spray, a column of white vapour rising high into the sky and floating away (as I saw it last night from a distance) like a summer cloud. Imagine all this, and you have still the weakest and faintest idea of Niagara.

I speak chiefly of the Main or Horseshoe Fall, be-

tween Canada and Goat Island, over which Fall, I
suppose, at least three-fourths of the river runs.   It
is well named the "Horseshoe" for it is much of that
shape.

The Fall between Goat Island and the American
main land is the finest Fall, *per se*, next to Schaff-
hausen, I ever saw ; but it is not to be compared to
the "Horseshoe," from which it is separated by some
300 or 400 yards of the dark cliffs of Goat Island.
That Island is from 50 to 100 acres in extent, prettily
wooded, and well looked after, affording admirable
points from which to view the Rapids above the
Falls and the Falls themselves.   I am told that it is
private property; if so, its owner deserves the thanks
of all nations, not alone for the opportunity he gives
to the public of enjoying this wonderful scene ; but
even more because he appears to have resisted the
seductions of those who desire to use the vast power
developed by this Fall.

Above the American Fall there are several hideous
mills, but the great Fall is disfigured and desecrated
by no such base use.   It is still as Nature made it—
one of her most wonderful works.

Below the Falls the river is enclosed in a precipitous gorge; the channel is very narrow, but it is said
to be from 300 to 600 feet deep, and it must indeed
be so to contain such a volume of water in a width
of not more than 120 yards.

At first the water flows calmly along in its deep
channel, but at the distance of about a mile it again
rushes madly through the gorge, and for some hun-

dreds of yards is dashed into waves of almost Atlantic dimensions. It then enters an open space called the Whirlpool, from whence it flows away through its gorge, forming further rapids, until it reaches the placid depths of Lake Ontario, and issues forth as the great St. Lawrence.

It is curious to reflect on the physical causes of this great cataract. The inland seas of North America, Lakes Superior, Michigan, Huron, and Erie, lie on a vast plateau far above the sea level. This plateau ends in an abrupt escarpment at a short distance from Lake Ontario, which escarpment we see stretching in a continuous line along the banks of that lake. It consists of horizontal strata, much resembling our Lias in its lithological character; but I could find no fossils to guide me, and I see by my map that it belongs in reality to the Silurian formation. If any Glamorganshire man will think of the Lias cliffs along the coast at Dunraven, St. Donat's, and Southerndown, and imagine the level of that plateau to represent the drainage level of a million square miles to the North, and that all the water which falls thereon were gathered together in one mighty river, and launched sheer over the cliff, he will have a fair idea of the physical conditions which create these great Falls.

I had the theory of the measurement of the world's age by the retrogression of these falls much in my mind, but for various reasons, too long to detail now, I entirely disbelieve it.

The recollection of the first day spent in presence

of this most wonderful development of one of Nature's greatest forces must ever remain deeply graven on my memory, and indeed, a second visit in no way diminished the intensity of my first impression.

A few hours sufficed for Toronto, which can claim no special notice. It is well built and prosperous, but not progressive. It values itself especially on being the chief seat of learning of the Dominion. It possesses a fine range of University buildings, with a good staff of Professors and adequate endowments, in fact the University of Toronto is the principal one of Canada.

Toronto supplies a large district with goods of all kinds, but it is not distinguished like Montreal for its commercial activity. The situation of the City on the shores of Lake Ontario is more like that of a Dutch town, flat and altogether devoid of interest.

Hamilton, at the Western end of the Lake, though younger and rougher, is far more vigorous. Besides being the Swindon of the Great Western Railway of Canada, it possesses two special manufactures, " Stoves and Sewing machines," and many of its inhabitants are growing rapidly rich by these industries. The well-known " Wanzer" sewing machine is manufactured here. In good times 300 hands are employed, now only 100, so greatly does even this industry suffer from the bad times.

The manufacture of stoves is of much importance in this rigorous climate. Great improvements have been made, and they are well worthy of our attention in England, and especially in North-West Glamorgan.

The essential feature of the Hamilton stove is that it is a self-feeder, depending on Anthracite for its success. It is lighted in the Autumn, and put out in the Spring, burns but little coal, gives but little trouble, and throws out a great and uniform heat. I believe that much economy would result from the use of these stoves, especially if placed in the passages and entrances of our houses, the pipes being carried through the living rooms into the chimneys. My hostess, a most sensible Lancashire lady, long resident at Brecon, which she only left two years ago, is loud in her praises of Canadian stoves— perfect comfort in winter and no heavy coal bills, instead of just the reverse in the old country. If we wish to enjoy that special pleasure of an Englishman, poking the fire, and to preserve the health undoubtedly due to the ventilation produced by our open fire-places, we may still do so ; but there is no reason why we should not be warm, or why those who can't afford to waste coal should for ever go on doing so. We possess the finest anthracite in the world, and it lies almost unworked. It would be well if our anthracite coal proprietors would push the Canadian stove ; and if any desire to do so, I shall be too glad to show them those I have ordered, which I hope to have in full blast before Christmas.

Hamilton possesses a good market ; the prices current in this Canadian town may not be uninteresting, in view of the sending of dead meat to England—a problem now being rapidly solved. I shall do no more than touch on it, however, as Canada

G

will not be the source from whence the chief supplies will come to England. When at Chicago I hope fully to investigate this important question. I visited the market at Hamilton and received the following replies :—Beef, 4d. to 6d. per lb. for the best pieces, inferior pieces much less, stock meat almost given away ; mutton, 3d. per lb. ; lamb, 3¾d. per lb. ; a couple of fine chickens, 2s. 6d., and other poultry in like proportion. These prices were retail. The meat was excellent : I never saw finer mutton and lamb. There was the carcase of a sheep hanging up (a cross between a Leicester and Southdown), which would have done credit to the Vale of Glamorgan.

But it is not from the restricted lands of Canada, which do not produce more than enough for the consumption of the country, that supplies will come to England. The vast prairies of the west, where I am told cattle roam in countless herds, are destined to supply the wants of England. I learnt at Boston that about one penny per pound will deliver meat from Chicago to Liverpool, all told, and that the first cost is from 4d. to 5d. ; but, as I said before, I will defer this question till I can deal with it on the spot.

While travelling to Toronto, I was introduced to an ex-official of the Dominion, who was returning from a tour in the far north-west of Canada. He told me that he had visited the farm of a Scotchman, I think in "Manitoba," where he grows annually fifteen thousand acres of wheat. He goes there with his men and his teams, ploughs the land in furrows six miles long—one furrow out and home is a day's work,—sows and reaps his corn, clears off, and goes home in three months. Such an operation sounds fabulous in our ears, and I therefore give my authority. No doubt the virgin soil of the prairies is easily handled, and the seasons are wonderfully rapid. Except near the coast, I have not seen a particle of corn standing—all carried, and some thrashed. No portion of the country I have yet seen (and I have already travelled over thousands of miles) admits of such dashing operations. All that I have 'seen has been won by hard toil from the forest. In much the stumps still stand, much is still unreclaimed, much is so rocky as to be irreclaimable; but I believe the prairie land is quite different. Thus far I have been surprised to see how little good farming exists in the oldest settlements; but I am told that in north-western Ontario the land and farming are excellent.

Apples, pears, and peaches are abundant in this part of Canada. The apples unrivalled, the pears execrable; I have not ate a really good one yet. Singularly enough nectarines do not flourish, nor do apricots and plums. Gooseberries damp off. Currants, strawberries, and raspberries are abundant. Tomatos are grown like potatoes. Why not also with us? The latter are excellent in spite of the Colorado beetle, which I now and then meet walking about like an innocent insect, not at all sensible of the noise he is making in the world. No one mentions his name here, but I was told when at Boston that they had crossed one of the streets in such numbers as almost to stop the traffic. I did not see them, and cannot vouch for the truth !!!

The task of going minutely into every detail of a line of railway 900 miles in length, and complicated by all kinds of diplomacy, detains my friend at Hamilton. Well were it for all foreign undertakings made with English gold if their chairmen would pay them a yearly visit and devote six weeks of patient energy and self-denying toil to their concerns. Fewer half-pay officers, widows, and orphans would have their hopes of high interest blasted, and find their straightened means still more straightened, if such were the rule. However, the Great Western of Canada is a fortunate exception, and a fortnight more must be spent at Hamilton before we can take our flight for our long journey " out west."

So we resolve on a trip to the States in the mean-time. A night in a Pullman lands us at 6 on a lovely Sunday morning at Albany, an ancient City, founded in 1612 on the banks of the Hudson, 150 miles above New York, numbering about 80,000 inhabitants, the capital of the State of New York and seat of its legislature. It has all the look of an " old town"—red brick houses and irregular streets, very good public buildings and really fine churches. I can vouch for singing not being neglected, for at St. Peter's, the chief Episcopal Church, I was sung to nauseam by a set of male and female minstrels who executed Venites, Te Deums, Jubilates and

Voluntaries, in every letter of the alphabet, I believe, from a pretentious organ gallery. I hope they sang praises for me as well as for themselves, for I confess my utter inability to take part in such services.

At an early hour on Monday (10th Sept.), we embarked for our steam down the Hudson on board the " C. Vibbard," one of those floating three decked castles I described before, propelled by a 65 inch cylinder engine, 12 feet stroke. Alongside her lay the St. John, the night boat, 85 inch cylinder and 15 feet stroke. The most powerful engine in Glamorganshire for any purpose is, I believe, an 80 inch pumping engine. This will convey some idea of the size of these steamers.

For at least one-third of the 150 miles from Albany to New York the Hudson did not impress me. Its banks are well wooded, undulating and fertile, but nowhere more than pretty—here and there a village ; here and there a farm ; much natural wood ; all hard wood, no fir. Even the Catskill Mountains, the scene of Rip-van-Winkle's exploits, seemed a tame and uninteresting range of rounded hills, something like the Malvern Hills, but not possessing such fine outlines.

Below Rhinbeck the scenery becomes much finer. The hills approach the river, which widens out into splendid reaches and then contracts to a few hundred yards. The reach above Newburg, bounded on the south by the " Highlands," which must be several thousand feet high, and surrounded by beautifully wooded slopes, is very striking. At first one does not see how the river escapes through the mountain chain, but gradually a narrow gorge comes in sight, with precipitous sides and winding course, in the centre of which upon a projecting promontory the famous Military Academy of West Point is situated, commanding the gorge with its batteries.

Issuing from the narrow ravine we soon enter on the fine Fjord called the Tappanzee, probably eight or ten miles long by four or five broad, its southern and western shores shut in by high precipitous mountains and bluff headlands, its eastern shore rising gently from the water, and thickly studded with the villas, almost country houses, of the rich New York merchants, embosomed in trees, and surrounded by well-kept lawns and parks. The same evidences of luxurious and happy country life continue on the eastern shore for many miles, until the busy quays of New York are reached, while the western shore is a wall of bold and lofty precipices called the " Palisades." I have never been more struck with any river scenery. Indeed, mile for mile, I have no hesitation in saying that I think the Hudson far finer than the finest parts of the Rhine. I would go further, and say that it has many of the attributes of our own Bay—a fine expanse of water, numbers of ships with their well-cut white sails gliding hither and thither, bold outlines near and far, lovely vegetation down to the water's edge ; all this lit by an Italian sun, rendered endurable by a fresh sea breeze. If ever I emigrate, which heaven forfend, it will be to the Hudson.

CHAPTER IV.

NEW YORK.

IT would indeed be the height of presumption to attempt any description of New York after spending three days there. Every child knows that it is the chief City of the United States,—that it is called the "Empire City," and does in fact exert Parisian influence throughout the whole domain of the Union. To fathom and define the intricacies of its political ramifications, whether "Unionic" (if I may be allowed to coin a word), State, or Municipal, would require probably more than the acuteness of the editor of the *New York Herald.* To study and describe its public institutions would be a work of years; to detail its social arcana would need the opportunities and pens of Pepys or Greville. But even the hasty sketch possible after a three days' glance, every statement to be taken with the classic "grain of salt," may be of some interest.

Physically, at any rate, New York is easily described; and a magnificant physical position it occupies, covering as it does a long, narrow island, surrounded on three sides by water, deep enough to float a line of battle-ship at low tide, completely land-locked, and yet at a short distance from the Atlantic—about 20 miles—easily accessible chan-

nels, with 21ft. to 22ft. at dead low water, 27ft. to
29ft. at high tide. No enormous expenditure is
required to create locks, docks, quay walls, piers,
breakwaters, harbours of refuge, and the like. Its
wharves are formed by simply driving piles at right
angles to the shore, and boarding over the space
thus gained from the sea. It is evident that while
such frontage may be indefinitely extended along
the shores, it may equally be run out at right angles
to almost any extent; and that little or no capital
being required to create floating accommodation,
small interest has to be paid, and the lightest possible
dock dues suffice. Vessels also can come in and go
out when they please,—no detention occurs from
want of water at low tide.

New York was further favoured by her splendid
inland water communication before the days of railroads, the Hudson River and Erie Canal forming at
that time the means of transporting heavy goods,
thus making her the outlet for the produce of vast
districts at her back.

No one can contemplate the eastern, western, or
southern portions of New York harbour, whatever
his experience of the Thames, the Mersey, or the
Clyde may be, without feelings of astonishment and
admiration. The movement of shipping is so
perpetual that it almost seems as if the whole
surface of those sheets of water was as overcrowded
as our London thoroughfares. Steamers of all sorts
and sizes, sailing craft, barges, but, above all, the
enormous ferry-boats dash about and drift about in

all directions. The ferry-boats are wonders in themselves. I had the curiosity to take the dimensions of one, and found it to be 225 ft. long, and 60ft. broad, driven by a 58in. cylinder engine, 12ft. stroke. The centre is occupied by carts, waggons, carriages, and railway trucks, and the sides by covered ways and saloons for foot passengers, the whole roofed over from end to end. Dozens of these may be seen ploughing their way over New York harbour to Brooklyn, New Jersey, Hoboken, &c. Before further bridges are built across the Thames, it will be well to see if every object could not be attained by such commodious ferry-boats ; and even Liverpool, with her broad Mersey, has much to learn from her twin sister on this side.

The business part of New York is much like the business parts of our large towns,—perpetual noise and bustle, streets too narrow for the work to be done, open doors with rows of names within, and the modern extravagance in office and warehouse building ; dressed-stone fronts, some even of white marble ;· rich-carved architraves, polished granite columns, Corinthian and Moorish capitals ; and inside perhaps " skeletons" carefully nursed in many a banker's parlour. Numbers of them have now been swept out, and may not so easily be allowed to re-enter. The storm which has swept over the world for three long years came from America. Let us pray that the gleam of sunshine now seen here for the first time may re-invigorate us, and start us into fresh life, not, however, we trust of such unhealthy

H

tropical luxuriance, but the sturdy growth of temperate climes.

If we pass from the bustle of Wall-street and the south end of Broadway, and pursue that long thoroughfare steadily towards the north, we find a marked change as we leave each "block" behind us. Great shop-fronts succeed to offices, and we soon see the ways and means by which the money, made by the sweat of men's brows in the south, is wasted by their gentle mates in the northern end of the same street, which, I am bound, however, to admit, is said to be some five miles long. If we turn to the left, into the renowned "Fifth Avenue," we still further see how the costly tissues of Broadway are dragged through the filth by the vanity of woman, as if she desired to prove that Darwin is after all right, and that a three feet trail is needed to complete the attractions of her form divine. Why are our strong sense Anglo-Saxon dames led to ape the follies of their Gallic prototypes? Why do they allow the latter always to set the fashion? The great Mr. Worth assured me last Easter, when I twitted him with this ungainly folly of tight-tied dresses and draggle trails, that he highly disapproved, and did all he could to stop it. Mr. Worth is the setter of Paris fashion, and a sound-hearted Lincolnshire man, and yet the ladies beat him.

What has this to do with New York? Oh, "Fifth Avenue!" Well, that street is Belgravia, Kensingtonia, Tyburnia, and the parts about St. James's, Berkeley, Grosvenor, and all other Squares rolled into one long street, with some cross satelites. The houses are mostly three-windowed, and from 25 ft. to 35 ft. frontage,—about the same height as ours,—some are really fine houses, but each such has a history which, as we rumbled along, was duly imparted.

There was the house of the Astors, which recalled to my mind stories I had read of the adventurous merchant who fitted out his expeditions to the Far West, then unknown, in search of peltries, and, in competition with the Hudson's Bay Company, was the patron of a thousand trappers whose deeds fill the pages of romance. Then there was Vanderbilt's mansion, the king of American railroads. I gave 2 min. 14 sec. as the time in which the father trotted a mile, with one horse. The son has just done the mile in the shortest time on record with a pair of horses, viz., 2 min. 23 sec., his bet being that he would do the mile with a pair under 2 min. 25 sec., thus attaining the speed of 25 miles an hour.

Last, not least, there was the white marble mansion, with its gold facings, the abode of the late "dry goods" salesman, A. T. Stewart, who died last year, leaving a fabulous sum. "Dry goods" mean Shoolbreds, Harveys, Whiteley and Co., and it seems to be the most prosperous of all businesses both here and at home. The houses in Fifth Avenue fetch a higher price, house for house of equal frontage, than in the fashionable parts of London.

At the end of Fifth Avenue is the Park, and it

well deserves that name, for it is upwards of 800 acres in extent. The surface is what the French well call "accidenté," i.e., broken into hill and valley on a miniature scale. Advantage has been taken of every natural feature. The hill has its circular plateau, from which fine views are obtained; the hillsides have their groves and shady walks; the valleys their small lakes. Well-kept drives and "rotten rows" lead hither and thither; and even when we were there, before the return of the gay world, there were fair numbers of carriages, and especially the typical light trotting buggy in which the citizen delights to trot his better half about—I do not mean in the shafts, but gravely sitting by her side, and holding his boring horse with separate outstretched arms, not as the old mail coachman used to tell me when I was indulged with the ribbons, "Old 'em, sir, so as no one could tell you was a 'olding of 'em; sit back, and square yer sholders." The Yankee sits as if the next pull must take him off his seat on to his nag's ears. But for lightness, their carriages are masterpieces. We are in the days of our grandfathers. Peters, Barker, Ward and Co. have yet to learn what a carriage is, and how to build it. We make our horses drag weights which are wholly unnecessary, because we do not know how to use materials properly. I was driven over some roads in New Jersey which would have shaken any of my carriages to pieces, but the new Jersey waggon, holding six, went over them like a spider, and as easily as a C and underspring barouche.

And this reminds me of that lovely drive along a ridge of high ground, finely wooded with oak and chestnut, close above Sandy Hook, at the entrance of New York harbour, from which we looked down on the broad expanse of New York Bay, studded with a thousand sails, with Staten Island, Long Island, and the Narrows in the distance, and the great Atlantic away beyond the narrow neck of Sandy Hook ; inland, a lovely wooded country, broken into hill and dale, the last of the old entailed properties of New Jersey,—one of the most lovely views I ever enjoyed. For this afternoon's pleasure we have to thank a kind friend to whom we had letters, and who invited us to stay with him at his country house in New Jersey, the quiet and refinement of which was a most agreeable break to the racket of constant Hotel life. It also gave us the opportunity of steam-ing down the whole length of New York harbour to Sandy Hook. Those who attempt to force its entrance will receive hard blows if the batteries we passed are well armed and manned.

The growth of New York has been marvellously rapid. It is said, with Brooklyn, Jersey City, and its immediate suburbs, to have nearly 2,000,000 inhabitants ; 180 years ago it had but 6,000 ; and 260 years ago it had none at all. Brooklyn is as much part of New York as Lambeth is of London, and before long it will be connected with it by a grand suspension bridge.

I see it stated that New York has 334 places of worship, of which 73 are Protestant Episcopalian, 55

Presbyterian, 45 Methodist Episcopalian, 39 Roman Catholic, 30 Baptist, 27 Jewish, 18 Reformed Dutch, 13 Lutheran, 5 Congregational, 4 Unitarian, 4 Universalist, and 18 miscellaneous. Many of these churches are in most respects magnificent structures, especially the Roman Catholic Cathedral which is built of white marble, but is still unfinished. Each Denomination seems to vie with the other in the construction of " temples exceedingly beautiful." The old prejudices as to the conventicle form have passed away. No man can say as he passes an American church to what Denomination it is likely to belong.

A good story is told at Toronto upon this point. A well-known English Peer recently visited Toronto, and was lionised by a rich Banker. Among other things of interest he was shown a very fine new Gothic church, and he moralized somewhat in this strain :—" How satisfactory it is to see the vigour with which our ancient Church sustains her position in our colonies without adventitious aid." " But," the Banker quietly remarked, " this is a Nonconformist place of worship, my Lord," to which the Peer replied, " Pshaw ! so like the arrogance of those Dissenters." The Banker, who was a member of the congregation, and had contributed 20,000 dollars to the church, made no reply, but told it with much amusement to his friends, and it is now a standing joke at Toronto.

Many of the churches are built in the 13th and 14th century style. but some have a style of their own.

I have long thought it was unworthy of our age to
copy as we do so servilely the style of those centuries, and I have wondered that our architects did
not strike out some types of their own not quite so
hackneyed. I am bound to say that this reproach
does not lie at the door of the Americans, who have
struck out a style of their own, while retaining many
of the best features of our Gothic buildings. Their
masonry is more massive, the members of their
window traceries are heavier and bolder, they splay
out their towers and buttresses, they introduce tur-
retted angles instead of plain quoins, their spans are
larger, and conceptions generally bolder than ours.
I am convinced that the cost of these churches
must be great, and it speaks well for the religious
feelings of Americans that they devote such sums
to these objects.

Philadelphia, where I am now writing, is said to
contain 419 churches, and I can testify to the substantial and handsome exterior of many : 91 Presbyterian, 75 Episcopalian, 38 Roman Catholic. Only
15 are credited to the sect of the famous founder of
the city, William Penn. I mention these numbers
to convey some notion, however imperfectly, of the
relative preponderance of various sections of the
Christian Church. I have been told that throughout the United States the Baptists are numerically
the strongest, while the Episcopalians are the
richest.

There is little to be said of a fugitive character
about Philadelphia ; much, I doubt not, if one had

time to study it ; but here again the extremely short
time I can allot to each object of interest intervenes,
and, moreover, I have not had the advantage of asso-
ciating with those who could give me rapidly the information I could desire, for the majority of Philadelphians are away, and not one of those to whom I
have letters is to be found.

Philadelphia ranks next to New York among the
cities of America, numbering about 800,000 inhabitants. In 1777 it had 21,000 ; in 1800, 70,287. The
site of Philadelphia was well chosen. The junction
of two such rivers as the Schuylkill and the Dela-
ware would alone suffice to endow it with facilities
of water communication and picturesque features
not possessed by ordinary cities. But still more
important is its proximity to the Atlantic, being
about 100 miles distant, and accessible to large
vessels at high tide; while the great Coalfield at its
back adds materially to its commercial and manufacturing importance.

In the fashionable quarter I see many houses
quite equal to the best in New York. One special
feature gives Philadelphia a distinctive character ;
white marble appears to be almost its cheapest
building stone. The doorsteps of fourth or fifth-rate
houses are of white marble, and many house-fronts
are wholly made of it, as also quoins and dressings,
worked in with a very fine red brick. This imparts
to the place a singularly clean and bright appearance.
Granite is also largely used, as well as a sandstone
of a deep red colour, and a drab freestone—I imagine

New Red and Permian; the white marble is probably "altered Jura," or Oolite like Carrara; but I have quite failed to get a geological map. Gneiss crops up in the Park at the Water Works, and Silurian further on. Nothing is more striking in the Canadian and American Cities, that I have visited, than the variety and good quality of their building stone.

Philadelphia, like most American Cities, is built in squares or "blocks" of houses; the streets running north and south are numbered consecutively, beginning at the River, so that each succeeding street is a number higher than the preceding one ; thus, if your friend lives in Forty-fifth street, you know that he is forty-five blocks from the river. Each block is supposed to contain 100 houses, but really contains only from 60 to 70 ; in spite of this deficiency the numeration proceeds on the theory of 100, and thus a simple calculation will always inform you where a house is, the number of the street being known ; thus, my hotel is in Broad or Fourteenth Street ; now all the streets which cross it at right angles will have 1401 on one side and 1402 on the other, until the next, or Fifteenth Street is reached, when they will begin with 1501—1502.

The streets crossing at right angles are here called after trees ; thus Walnut and Chestnut Streets are the two principal east and west streets. Chestnut Street is full of fine shops, equal to those of any city I ever visited. The old " State Hall," or " Independence Hall," is most interesting to Americans, for in it was signed the famous Declaration

I

of Independence; the table, chair, and inkstand used
on the occasion are still shown; from the broad
steps of its facade the Independence of the United
States was proclaimed.

The portraits of those who took part in the revolutionary war are hung round the Hall, while in the
adjacent room are original pictures of Charles II.,
George II., George III., William Penn, &c., with
many relics of the war of independence. Among
others they have an old cracked bell called "Liberty
Bell," which first rang out the pœan of the " Immortal Declaration." I thought it a fit emblem of the
uncertain sound which the word " Liberty" must
now convey to Americans: what with professional
politicians, wire-pullers, jobbers, and Presidential
" difficulties," the purity of public life seems to
have become a thing of the past, and the "Liberty"
of the community to govern themselves straight-
forwardly, seems sadly shattered. The majority
of sensible Americans know this in their secret
hearts, and would give much to get out of their
political difficulties.

The principal United States mint is here. It is a
well conducted establishment, now hard at work
evidently coining for a resumption of specie payments, and I fear especially in silver.

Philadelphia is a busy place; there are numerous
establishments for the manufacture of locomotives,
mechanical tools, iron of all description, textile fabrics,
carpets, and various other industrial products. The
main building of the Centennial Exhibition is still

standing, and, large as it is, Philadelphian manufacturers are almost able to refurnish it from their
multifarious workshops.

The exhibition building is really a fine structure,
better than any I have seen except our Crystal
Palace in 1851. It still contains much of interest,
and gives one a fair idea of what it must have been
last year. Its site adds much to its effect, placed as
it is on the confines of Fairmount Park, the most
lovely and extensive Park, so far as I know, of
which any city in the world can boast, containing
no less that 1617 acres, of which 170 represent the
water area of the Schuylkill—a broad and fine river,
with rocky banks rising 100 feet and upwards from
its margin, now approaching close and now receding,
covered with a fine growth of natural forest trees,
many of considerable age and size, with grassy glades
and luxuriant vegetation. The roads are broad and
well kept, and paths are carried in all directions.
Near the town the ground is laid out in parterres
and ornamental gardens, while the more distant
portions are allowed to retain their natural characteristics. The reaches of the river remind me of the
Thames above Maidenhead; but the Schuylkill is
wider, and the banks more broken and varied. At
both ends the gorge is spanned by railway bridges
of a very ornamental and light construction.

At the town end the water works are well worthy
of a visit. A weir dams back the river to a height
of 14 feet at low and 6 feet at high tide. Five
tourbines of 10 ft. 3 in. diameter work powerful

pumps, and force the water up to a reservoir constructed on an isolated outburst of gneiss, some
acres in extent, giving a high service to the City at
a trifling cost comparatively.   When I first saw it I
thought how fortunate are the Philadelphians as to
their water supply.   But I drive through their
beautiful Park, and along the bank of their broad
River, and what do I see on the high ground above
me ?   Is it possible, or is it a ghastly dream ?
I see white marble tombstones in thick array.   It is
their great Laurel Hill Cemetery, with its adjuncts,
covering 130 acres of ground, 110 feet above the
river which supplies their town with water, the
graves I should judge within little more than 50
yards of the water's edge.   And this Cemetery
receives a large proportion of the dead of 800,000
people.   Rain falls on it : where does it soak to ?
and where does it afterwards drain to ?   The thought
is too hideous to pursue ; but if I were a Philadelphian I should look askance at my iced water, and
my tea would lose its charms.   I should say, " At
once lay in pipes higher up the river than the
drainage level of the Cemetery, and conduct pure
water to the pumps, or else remove the pumps bodily
higher up the river.

I am sorry to pick a hole in such pretty combinations as the Park, the Cemetery, and the Water
Works, but " honesty obliges."   I passed hundreds
of light trotting carriages to-day full of happy Cits,
with their wives and children, dashing all unconsciously along the well kept roads.   I saw thousands

walking and sunning themselves in the trim gardens, and by the pretty fountains. What if the destroying angel, in the shape of typhoid and cholera, or other plague, now clearly shown to be transmissible by infected water supplies, struck these happy people through their grave-yard and their river, and the thought had occurred to me, and I had not spoken it out ! !   Good-bye Philadelphia : no more iced water for me within your borders.

I am off to Pittsburg, the Merthyr of America, but my iron and coal friends must not be disappointed if I do not give them a chapter on " costs and yields," or the latest American inventions.   My time is short, and between this and San Francisco lie Chicago, Utah, Denver, Colorado, and many a thousand miles, more novel and interesting to me than iron works and collieries.   If time permits as I return, perhaps I may re-visit this district with a carbon and metallic mind.

CHAPTER V.

PITTSBURG.

THE journey by the Pennsylvania Central Rrilway from Philadelphia to Pittsburg, 355 miles, by day Express, in 12 hours, is by no means without interest. The first portion of it is through a highly-farmed country, which reminded us much of England, more so than any district we have yet passed through. The fields are large, with substantial post and rail fences. There is much fine timber, and here and there woods—quite as much woodland, in fact, as in any part of England. The country is prettily broken into hill and dale. The houses and steadings have a neat and cared-for look. Orchards abound, laden with fruit. In fact, were it not for the fields of Indian corn and tobacco, one might fancy oneself travelling through a pretty English county.

The latter portion of the line is wilder, and reminded me of some Continental scenery, but I cannot exactly remember where,—I think the approaches to the Jura from the French side, or the southern slopes of the Hartz mountains.

After passing Harrisburg, 107 miles from Philadelphia, the line crosses the Susquehanna, at this point,—a broad, shallow, lacustrine river,—by a bridge 3,670 feet long, winding its way through a

mountain ridge about 1,000 feet to 2,000 feet high,
clothed with natural wood to the summit.   It then
enters the valley of the Juniata, a confluent of the
Susquehanna, the course of which it follows for about
100 miles between hills of the same type, somewhat
like the Neath and Taff Vales; no bold peaks, but
rounded skylines, broken here and there by lateral
dingles.   These are the spurs of the Alleghanies,
which are crossed further on at Altoona.   They are
said to be very beautiful, but darkness came on just
as we reached them.   The moon was bright, however,
and I confess it seemed to me that the scenery continued much the same as before.   I could always see
the skyline at no great height until we reached
Pittsburg, which certainly is not Merthyr the smokeless, but Sheffield the unctuous and smutty, for it
lives under that pall of black smoke in which our
Admiralty delights to envelope its fleets, when it
goes to the North for its coal supplies.

The sounds of exhaust steam, counter flies, pinions,
steam hammers, hooters, and all other adjuncts of
Tubal Cain's calling, were the music of the night,
and, when day broke, the broad Monongahela River,
with its Suspension Bridge of many piers, and its
coal-laden barges, towed by sternwheel steamers
lashed alongside, appeared flowing past our windows,
while opposite was a precipice 470 feet high, rising
almost perpendicularly from the river at a distance
of perhaps 80 yards from its banks; but on that
narrow strip of flat land, and as far as could be seen
along the river banks, iron, steel, glass, and other

works are perched, vomiting forth so thick a volume
of black smoke as to render the cliffs opposite almost
invisible.   Higher up the river the cliffs recede, and
some of the largest works, as well as a considerable
population find their "location," as an American
would say, on the banks of the Monongahela, which
also conveys a large portion of the coal from the collieries to Pittsburg.   Other works are situate along
the proper left bank of the Alleghany River, which
unites with the Monongohela, and forms the Ohio
within the limits of the City.

Up the steep cliff opposite runs a passenger incline
at an angle of at least 45 deg., worked by a stationary
engine on the top.   If we pay six cents., in two or
three minutes we are pulled up to the top of the cliff,
and look down on the city from an elevation of 470
feet.   On our right and left at our feet is the
Monongahela River.   Opposite, on a tongue of land
gradually widening, and rising as it widens, eventu-
ally to an equal elevation with our own, is the city
of Pittsburg, enveloped in perpetual darkness under
its canopy of unctuous smoke.   Over the lower lying
houses, and far away towards the East, we see the
broad Alleghany River, while to the extreme left we
see the junction of these not inconsiderable rivers
uniting to form the great Ohio, destined in its turn,
after a course of many hundreds of miles, to be ab-
sorbed and lost in the mighty Mississippi.

Above the town, and out of reach of the smoke,
the country is extremely pretty.   It is laid out in
wide wood-paved roads, of which I was told there

are upwards of 30 miles, and upon which not less
than one million sterling has been expended, the
most lavish expenditure of public money I ever saw.
The paving is as good as Piccadilly, and the roads
nearly double the width.   The result of this and
other outlays for drainage, water, &c., is that the
local taxation of Pittsburg is excessive.   I make it
to be about equal to 3s. 10d. in the £, assuming
that a rebate of two thirds of the gross value is
allowed.   Thus the assessment is 3½ per cent. on
realised capital,—whether personal or real I omitted
to ask, but we will assume the latter.   Then, if a
man lives in a house which cost £1,000, we will
assume that he is assessed at £330, upon which he
would pay £11 10s. per annum.   If we put house
property at 6 per cent., his rent would be £60, upon
which he would pay £11 10s. or 3s. 10d. in the £
rental.   I have assumed one third because I found
that that was the proportion assessed in some other
American Cities.   The moral is, that no one need
emigrate to escape local taxation, and that corporate
bodies are no more exempt from extravagance and
expensive blunders on this than on the other side of
the Atlantic.   Philadelphia, the refined, expends
her money to pump up the drainage of her grave-
yard, and gives it to her people to drink.   Pittsburg,
the grimy, expends a million on roads, which would
be extravagent in London, and along which not one
in a hundred of her population passes.

    From the time I first landed I have enquired,
whenever I had an opportunity, as to " local taxa-

                                            K

tion," and I have heard the same story everywhere,
—bitter complaints of its burthen.   Yesterday I
spent some hours at the small town of London in
Canada.   They have no water supply even, but
their local burthens are 1·7 per cent., or nearly half
as much as at Pittsburg.

In the suburbs, accommodated by these magnificent
roads, the wealthy Pittsburg manufacturers have
their villas.   I drove through some miles of them,
and very comfortable English-like homes they seem
to be—nicely kept gardens, well mown grass plots
watered by small moveable fountains, croquet
grounds upon which "husbandry" seemed to be as
actively pursued as in the early days of that dull
game in England, and bright parterres of flowers.

The chief industries of the place are iron, steel,
and glass, the two former expanding into various
incidental manufacturers.   I visited the largest iron
works, but it was "standing," owing to a strike for
a 25 per cent. advance of wages, which had lasted
five weeks.   The product of this works is "merchant
bar" iron.   The manager came from Lord Dudley's
"Round Oak" Works.   I saw nothing new, except
the boilers and cold rolling of machine shafting.
The boilers universally adopted are of small diameter
in the shell, viz., 4ft. to 4ft. 4in., with two tubes
14in. to 16in., 24ft. to 30ft. long; shell plate $\frac{1}{4}$;
tubes plates, 5-16lbs.   In these boilers they carry
80lbs. to 120lbs. steam.   They are set, so to say,
"hollow," *i.e.*, they have no brickwork about them,
but are supported at the two ends only, the fire

underneath, and two or more boilers in a set. The flame returns through the flues. So far as I know, such boilers are not in use in England, and as they have all the elements of economy in consumption of coal, I mention them especially. I am also not not aware that machine shafting, up to 5in. diameter, is anywhere rolled cold with us. The saving is great, as the shaft leaves the rolls fit for use withou. the very expensive process of turning in a lathes They of course require straightening in pressure machines. My only doubt is whether the cold rolling may not render them too hard and brittle.

I also visited an extremely well conducted steel works, on the old system of mixing in pots. I could not learn that there were any Bessemer works at Pittsburg, although there are 15 in America,—the largest I believe at Troy, on the Hudson above Albany. Pittsburg goes in for merchant steel, not for heavy rails. At this works a very high quality of soft or malleable steel was being made. Although I saw many things which interested me, I can call to mind none of general interest, except perhaps the fact that in one department they were doing all the work with black men,— puddling and hammering. There were but two exceptions—the " boss," or foreman (every foreman is called a " boss" here), and the engineer. I asked the owner of the works, " What wages the black men earn ?" He replied, " I pay them by the same scale as the white puddlers; I would not ask them to work for less." He added, they were more easily

K 2

managed and more willing than white puddlers;
that if there was a press of work, they would take
out seven heats when a white man would knock off
at five; and that, "when working piece-work, Blackie
never heard the steam hooter or signal to cease working." I asked "If they stood heat better than white
men?" He said, "Neither better nor worse." A
portion of the local Press used to abuse him, and call
them "Jim Parks' black birds," but Jim Parks is
master of the situation, and don't care what they
call him, and he is quite right. He employs large
numbers of men, with whom he is on the best of
terms; he allows no drunkenness or disorder on the
one hand, and has a well-organised system of rewards
for good work on the other.

I also visited a large mill for rolling heavy double
T girders used in building houses, bridges, &c. The
conditions of manufacturing at Pittsburg are very
favourable. Coal is good and extraordinarily cheap.
"Through and through," an excellent rubbly coal,
with very little dead small, is only worth 90 cents,
for 2,000lbs. delivered in the works, as nearly as possible 4s. per ton. With this coal they can puddle
and do any work whatsoever. The best screened
coal is worth a dollar and a quarter, say 5s. 7d. per
2,000lbs; and slack 30 cents., or 16¾d. per 2,000lb.
The quality of the coal is quite equal to our Midland
or North Country Coal, very hard and cubical in its
fracture, bituminous and binding. I saw splendid
metallic looking flaky coke made from it. The
ash-pits showed that the coal was clean; in fact, I

should judge that it is quite equal to our bituminous coal. Wages vary from one dollar (4s.) for unskilled, up to four dollars for skilled, labour per day. A puddler gets three dollars, but he has to work for it· Under these conditions, and an abundance of the finest iron ore, I cannot see why Pennsylvania should not compete in its iron industry with us; but it has the curse of protection upon it, and where man interposes his short-sighted laws, the best provisions of Providence are shackled and blighted.

There is but one evil condition under which Pittsburg labours, as far as I could see, viz., its distance from a sea-port. Via Philadelphia it is 447 miles to New York. To Baltimore about 300 miles, but probably Cleveland on Lake Erie may become its best port, as it is only about 160 miles ; although Cleveland being a lake port can never compete with an Ocean port. It has a canal across the Alleganies, and the Rivers Ohio and Mississippi give it cheap freight to the South, but its main communication is by the Pennsylvania Central Railway, which has practically a monopoly, and makes the Pittsburgers pay for it ; in fact, the feeling roused against that line was to some extent the cause of the late riots, the lower classes having been excited against the railroad by much publicly expressed discontent.

It is now ascertained that property to the value of £500,000 in railway stock and merchandize was destroyed during the riots ; 1,600 railway waggons and their freight, 101 locomotives, and the whole of the stations, sheds, and engine houses were burnt

and wrecked. The State or district will have to pay.
Not a dollar's worth of private property was
destroyed.

It seems to have been a thoroughly mismanaged
affair,—a Militia Regiment from Philadelphia—having replied to a little stone throwing (and it is said
one pistol shot), by firing into a number of innocent
people, a large portion of whom were women and
children ; many were killed. These people had
collected innocently enough on a hill side to look at
the regiment ; the real strikers were across the line,
preventing trains from running, but the fight did
not begin with them. After this deed the Militia
marched away. The workmen, finding that women
and children had been killed, attacked and wrecked
the station and plundered the cars during the
following night. Many of these cars had spirits in
them, which were drunk *ad libitum*, and further in-
furiated the mob, but in all this drunkenness and
excess, private property was respected, and my
informant told me that the next morning he accompanied the Mayor, while he endeavoured to pacify
the mob, and that looking at them as they faced him
he could not see one steady workman among them.

In such a population (Pittsburg has 160,000 and
Allegany City on the other side of the river has
70,000) there are always roughs and bad characters
ready for any mischief, and those were the men,
and not the steady working classes who really caused
the riots. One company of Regulars soon put things
to rights.

The Regulars and Militia have different views of
their duty. I was told an anecdote which illustrates
this characteristically. A regular soldier on sentry
was pacing up and down among the wreck, when
some loafers got about him and tried to fraternise.
They said, " Now, if there was another row, you
would not shoot us, would you ?" He replied, " Not
shoot ! why d—— ye, I'm paid to shoot ! !" Rioters
and Regulars in America are much as they are with us.

From Pittsburg our route lay for twenty miles
along the banks of the Ohio, a fine river, here about
as wide as the Thames at London Bridge. We then
turned North, and followed the pretty valley of the
Beaver River for, I suppose, thirty or forty miles,
until it ceases to bear that name at the junction of
the Shenango and Mahoning Rivers, up the latter of
which the line to Erie is carried.

Throughout the whole of our journey we were passing through an extremely pretty country, well-farmed,
clearings alternating with natural woodlands, not an
acre of flat land, hill and dale in all directions. Much
of this country has a most park-like appearance, and
one fancied that at each turn a fine country house
would come in sight, but such things are not in
America. By and bye they may be, but not yet.

I saw that we were traversing a coal field. Here
and there we saw small workings, and from time to
time we passed good train loads of coal standing
on sidings ; but from the few openings we passed, and
the scanty population, it is evident that this district is
as yet almost untouched.

The coal measure sandstone reminded me of York-shire in its lithological character. We passed some considerable iron works, but most of the blast furnaces are idle; at one village, Sharpsville, the guard told me there were 13, and only two or three in blast; I also saw some extensive mills standing idle.

At last I have succeeded in getting a geological map, and I see we were traversing the northern portion of the great Pennsylvanian field, which extends far beyond the 41st to 33rd parallel of north latitude. Measured on the map it is 750 miles long and 180 miles wide at its northern end. At 350 miles south it is still 100 miles wide. For another 300 miles it is 40 miles wide, after which it widens out again to 100 miles, ending in the States of Alabama and Mississippi. If we contrast this with the South Wales coal field, which, I think, has the largest area in Great Britain, and so far as I remember is about 80 miles long and 25 wide at most, we shall have some conception of the enormous area of this great coal field; but the Kansas and Missouri coal field looks much larger. It seems to be 600 miles long, and an average of some 250 miles wide, while the Illinois field seems to be 300 miles long and 170 wide. What the quality of their respective coals may be I know not, but if all is as good and cheap as what I saw at Pittsburg, Providence would seem to have provided for the wants of countless millions of men during countless millions of ages.

I said in the discussion on the French Treaty, in the House of Commons, and I repeat, that the

production of coal is not measurable by the bountiful provisions of Providence, but by the hands
that can be brought to bear upon its working.
England has enough coal, and to spare, for a thousand
years. It would be presumptuous to speculate on
what America has, but its enormous wealth of coal
will be no more available until men can be found
to work it than if it had no existence ; it is a question
of men, not coal.

The great disadvantage under which America must
always labour, as a coal shipping country, is the
distance of the coal fields from the sea-board ; the
nearest point seems to be 150 miles from Baltimore as
the crow flies, probably 200 by rail. I am told upon
the highest authority that the rate per 2,000lbs. was
1¼ cents, but that owing to very keen competition it
is now reduced to ¾ of a cent per mile, or 6s. per 200
miles, or 6s. 8½d. per ton for delivery from the nearest
colliery to the port, a rate which we should consider
prohibitory. In Rhode Island and Massachusets there
is a small coal field on the sea ; it seems to be about
30 miles wide and 40 long, but with that exception
all the coal fields are inland.

Descending from the higher ground we soon found
ourselves on the shores of lake Erie, along which we
ran to Buffalo, the point at which the great Erie
canal begins, ending near Troy on the Hudson.

I have been agreeably surprised with everything
in Canada and America, except the great Lakes ;
those which I have seen have flat uninteresting
shores, while their very extent is so vast as to

L

produce no other effect than that of Seas. Anyone
who expects them to be like the Swiss or Italian
Lakes must be disappointed. The only place on the
Lakes I have seen, which is really striking, is Sarnia,
where I am now writing, at the Southern outlet
of Lake Huron. The waters of the great river,
here called the St. Clair, but really identical with
the Niagara and the St. Lawrence, rush past in a
grand volume 400 yards wide, and from 60 to 90
feet deep, at seven miles per hour, while a mile to the
North the apparently boundless expanse of Lake
Huron is seen. This in itself is fine, but the feature
of the place is the constant passage of large and
small craft, from the three-master of perhaps 400
tons, or the propeller of 500 or 600, down to the
coasting smack of 50 or 60 tons. Long lines of heavy
barges, in tow of powerful steamers, laden with grain
and timber, are perpetually passing. It must be
borne in mind that this is the only outlet to the
great Lakes, Superior, Huron, and Michigan, really
vast inland seas, from the shores of which immense
amounts of grain and lumber (*i.e.*, timber) are exported, and find their way to the sea, either *via* the
Erie Canal and the Railroad, or the Welland Canal,
from Lake Erie to Lake Ontario, and thence down
the St. Lawrence. This place, therefore, is as the
Bosphorus to the Black Sea, or the Belts to the
Baltic.

As I sit in this room, within 10 yards of the great
river, the rush of whose waters I hear, and along
whose rapid bosom this great trade is constantly

borne, I wonder at my ignorance, for I confess that until a few days ago I had no conception of the extent of the trade of these lakes, and no notion that such a place as Sarnia existed. The only thing I have ever seen like it is the view from the windows of the " Trafalgar " or the " Ship " at Greenwich, at high tide, on one of those delightful whitebait days when the mighty traffic of the world's mart is flowing by ; but here the sky is Italian and smokeless, and the sun powerful enough to make one seek the shade. This, indeed, is a truly delicious climate,—not one really bad day have we had since we landed five weeks ago,—and my letters tell me of floods, and crops destroyed at home.

A keen struggle for the Lake trade is now going on between the United States and Canada. In the former they are agitating for abolition of tolls on the Erie Canal, while Canada is constructing a splendid new system of lockage between Lakes Erie and Ontario, adjoining the old Welland Canal, which will enable vessels drawing, I believe, 18 feet or 20 feet of water to pass. Thus an 800 ton ship will be able to load in these inland seas, and discharge in our English ports. I think Canada will have the best of it ; and if so, it must greatly influence her future.

I must not omit to mention little " London," a thriving, vigorous little town, of 27,000 inhabitants, famous for its oil and beer. Mr. Carling's pale ale is equal to Bass or Allsop's. Mr. Waterman's manipulation of petroleum has gained him the highest prizes at all recent Exhibitions, even last year at Philadelphia, in competition with the great American producers. The oil wells are about 15 miles from " London," where the refining takes place. We spent some few hours yesterday at the works, but I will not attempt to describe the processes we saw. Anyone will find them far better given in my friend Mr. Hunt's last edition of Dr. Ure. London, like all Canadian Cites, is thoroughly loyal to the old country. It has Victoria and Westminster Bridges, Piccadilly, Pall Mall, and many other of the principal thoroughfares of its great namesake.

CHAPTER VI.

SARNIA.

No wonder that the constant passing and repassing of shipping at Sarnia produces a feeling of astonishment in the mind of a stranger, for I see that Secretary Sherman stated in a recent speech that "the whole tonnage passing at a given point on the line of the lakes is 3,000,000 tons per annum," or 10,000 tons per day, to which must be added the vessels in ballast.

From Sarnia we ran down to Toledo, and on our way we "struck a cow," not an uncommon occurrence in America, and attended with no such consequences as those which recently happened on the London and South Western, when several passengers were killed, and some injured. Every American locomotive is provided with a "cow catcher"—a wooden frame resembling a double plough (or, as it is spelt here "plow"), which removes any obstruction, and throws it on one side. Our cow was deposited in the ditch, and we did not feel the shock. There is no sort of reason why every locomotive in England should not have a proper cow-catcher. I have the opinion to that effect of a gallant officer, of all other men most competent to judge, having investigated more accidents in England than any other living man, and who also is well acquainted with American railways. If our railway companies will not voluntarily adopt obvious and proved means of safety, such as this and the pneumatic break system, with which every railway carriage in America is provided, they must be compelled by law to do so.

Toledo is a place of considerable importance, and rapidly progressing. In 1850 the population was under 4,000, and now it is 45,000. It is second only to Chicago in its grain exports. I was told that its export now amounts to 47,000,000 bushels annually, while it can store in its "elevators," as the great grain warehouses are called, 3,000,000 bushels. Eight railroads meet there, and two have their factories in the vicinity. The position of Toledo marks it out as a centre of commerce. It is situated near the mouth of the Maumee River, which, connecting with the Wabash, runs back between 300 and 400 miles, traversing part of Ohio and Indiana States. The Maumee River is deep enough at Toledo for ocean vessels, and as wide as the Thames at Westminster. In fact, vessels load grain here for Liverpool; when the Welland Canal improvements are completed, vessels up to 18ft. or 20ft. draft will be able to engage in the trade. It seems to me, therefore, that the position of Toledo is by far superior to Chicago.

A glance at the map will show that by sending grain from the West and South to Toledo instead of Chicago, the immense *détour* involved in sailing up the whole length of Lake Michigan and down Lakes

Huron and St. Clair will be saved, not to mention
the dangerous navigation of the Straits of Mackinaw.
I make the distance by the lakes about 650 miles,
against about 250 by rail; the produce of Indiana
and Illinois would not have to pass Chicago at all,
and an angle would be saved. I dwell upon this
as having an important bearing on the future of
the grain trade between England and America.
My present impression is that the port of Toledo on
Lake Erie must become the greatest grain-shipping
port of the United States; but when I get to Chicago
I may hear facts which may change my opinion.

Like other American towns, Toledo is laid out in
broad, straight streets, the business portion substantially and even handsomely built, while the suburban
roads are planted with double rows of trees, and
lined with handsome villas.

After spending a few hours at Toledo, I went on
to Cleveland, on Lake Erie. I was specially anxious
to visit it, as it is the lake port nearest to the
great Pennsylvanian coalfield, and a place of much
industry.

The line between Toledo and Cleveland runs
parallel to but at some distance from Lake Erie.
The country is flat and fertile; in fact, the whole of
this district is well farmed, and produces large quantities of grain. I say grain, because that word embraces all descriptions of cereals. Indian corn (called
here, *par excellence*, " corn") is largely grown
throughout this district, and I am told that in the
memory of man there has been no such harvest as

the present.   The farmers are generally satisfied
with 20 bushels to the acre, while this year they
have 45 bushels.

Even in this fertile district, at a rough guess, I
should say that not above two-thirds of the land is
cleared, the remainder being covered with natural
hard wood.   In many fields the stumps are still
standing.   Those who think that even in the oldest
settlement they will see great stretches of flat agricultural land, as in Germany and France, are mis-
taken.   I do not think I have been able to see more
than a mile or two from the train half-a-dozen times
since I have been in America.

Cleveland is situated on high ground on the
southern shore of Lake Erie, say 200 feet above
the Lake, which it overlooks.   It owes its origin to
the little River Ayahoga, which here enters the
Lake through a lateral valley with gently sloping
sides, and forms a port accessible to large vessels.
Piers are run out, with lighthouses at the end, and a
breakwater is about to be constructed, for this Lake
is a sea, nearly 300 miles long, and 50 wide.

The city was first settled by General Cleaveland
in 1796.   In 1830 it had 1,075 inhabitants, and now
I am told it has 160,000.   Steamers run from it to
every Lake port, and it has an important trade in
iron-ore from Lake Superior.   Being the nearest
port to the Pennsylvanian coalfield, I think it must
have a great future before it, both as an export and
import port.   The coalfield is only 20 miles distant,
at its extreme northern boundary, so that the lead

both outwards and inwards will be inconsiderable. The coal, however, which supplies the works at Cleveland, comes more than 100 miles by rail.

Cleveland has also canal communication traversing the coalfield, and ending only at the Ohio River. I observed that some of the largest iron works are on the banks of the canal, and it is probable that coal is brought cheaply to them by this means.

Cleveland boasts of some of the largest and best oil refineries in the States, as well as important steel, iron, screw, and other works. I visited the works of the " Otis Steel Company," having travelled from Swansea to London with its proprietor, who was returning from a visit to Landore. The works are new, and finished with every modern appliance for saving labour and turning out perfect work. Siemen's furnaces do all the melting and heating ; hydraulic pressure all the heavy labour. There was, therefore, a remarkable absence of the bustle, confusion, and dirt of an old-fashioned works. As the founder of the largest and best iron and steel works I ever saw, the late M. Schneider, who began and perfected the great Creusot Works, said to me not long before his death, and kept repeating, as having been his guiding rule in all his plans, " Chacun à son aise dans la moindre place possible," and that was the case in the " Otis Works." If we mean to keep our heads above water, we must avail ourselves of every means of saving fuel and labour, as well as of every practical scientific improvement.

The quality of the steel produced is quite A 1, but

M

then the materials they have at command here are
simply perfect,—billets of wrought iron made with
charcoal direct from the purest ore, without a trace
of any impurity.   The cost of coal is naturally higher
at Cleveland than at Pittsburg.   Small (but not dead
small) costs 135 cents., and large 190 cents. per
2,000lbs., or 6s. and 8s. $6\frac{1}{2}$d. per English ton.

I also visited the Union Screw Company's Works.
The machinery is excellent, entirely automatic.   Afterwards I drove round the town to the port and harbour,
and through the suburbs, which present the same
appearance of wealth and comfort which I have observed around every American town.   A description
of one will suffice for all, and I have seen none better
than Cleveland.   The streets of the town are broad,
and at right angles.   The chief street is 132ft. while
the minor streets are 100ft. broad.   Fine stone-built
houses five and six stories high, Banks, Stores (*i.e.*,
shops), Insurance Offices, State and Court-houses,
Post-offices, and the like, make up the centre of the
town, while works and factories line the routes of
through communication, such as canals, railroads, and
rivers.   The broad street soon fades off into a broad
avenue, consisting of a very wide road, having frequently two street-car tracks down the centre, and
often paved with wood ; then comes a solid stone
curb, say 1ft. wide ; then a well-cut grass verge, say
10ft. wide ; then a double avenue of hardwood trees,
beneath the inside of which runs the footpath ; then
a light iron railing, and sometimes none at all ; then
grass lawns, beautifully kept, with foliage plants,

sub-tropicals, and bedding-out stuff, in the midst of
which is the substantial Villa, generally six windows
to the front, quite detached, and, as to architecture,
"quot homines tot villæ"—one is no more like its
neighbour than the respective physiognomies of their
owners; but there is good Anglo-Saxon home comfort, and a well-to-do, happy look about each, be it
Grecian, Roman, or Snub.

As I drove along, I saw the fairer halves enjoying
rocking chairs and croquet, while their harder portions, like the poor niggers of old, " toiled all day"
in the store or office.   In the " Old Country," such
villas would cost from £2,000 to £10,000 each, and
the average run, £4,000 to £5,000.   It may be taken
as a rule that every American town has suburbs of
such Villas, more or less numerous and costly, according to the prosperity of the inhabitants.   I found
that the local rates of Cleveland are three per cent.,
but that the rateable value is only one-third of
the gross.   I had not time to visit a large Bessemer
steel works six miles distant, but I believe there is
nothing specially interesting about it.

My next day was spent at Detroit, another thriving port attached to Lake Erie, situated at the point
where the Great River, here called the " Detroit
River," leaves Lake St. Clair on its way to Lake
Erie.   The same immense traffic passes Detroit that
I saw at Sarnia, on its way to Buffalo, and the
Erie, or the Welland Canal.   At Detroit there are
some miles of wharves, at which ships of all sizes, up
to 500 tons, were lying, as well as large screw

steamers, engaged in the lake traffic. An extensive import timber business is carried on at Detroit for the supply of the district. Iron founderies, machine shops, and last, not least, copper works, were in active operation, the latter to melt the native copper of Lake Superior, a very simple smelting operation. Four furnaces working only in summer produce 6,000 tons per annum. The same company has a Works on Lake Superior consisting of eight furnaces, in which 15,000 tons per annum are produced, being a total of 21,000 tons of copper.

A friend who kindly accompanied me during part of my visit to Detroit said, " When I came here thirty years ago there were not 4,000 inhabitants, and now there are 120,000." I think this is somewhat more than the place looks like, but it is a most rising and important " city." It has public and private palatial offices, churches, and avenues of villas, not distinguishable by the eye of the ordinary visitor from those of the towns I have described. It is another of the coming cities.

The line from Detroit to Chicago passes through the best farmed country I have seen. For many miles the fields on both sides are under regular crops, corn and seeds. The winter wheat is now in many places showing above the ground, beautifully green and well drilled, the land as fine as a garden. The Indian corn is ripe, and in mows or ready to cut ; but everywhere woodlands abound, no doubt for fuel and shelter. Again and again I asked myself whether I could see a mile from the train, and, with one or

two exceptions, I was forced to return a negative
answer. We passed for the first 200 miles through
a gently undulating country, with here and there a
river shut in by wooded banks. We were now
running across the neck of the great Michigan
Peninsula, separating Lakes Huron and Michigan.

When we approached the latter, the country became flat and ugly, as on the shores of the other
great American lakes which I have thus far seen.
Huge banks of regular sea sand line the borders of
this inland sea at its southern end, rising as high as
any on the Atlantic coasts.

The latter portion of our route lay through a flat
and dreary country until we reached Chicago, the
capital of the West, now said to contain half a
million of inhabitants. Its development is perhaps
the most marvellous of any city on the American
Continent; but time will not now permit me to touch
upon it. I must reserve the slight sketch I may be
able to give of it until another mail. To-morrow
morning I embark " on board," as they say here, our
car for three days, three nights, and twelve hours, at
the end of which time we hope to land safely at Salt
Lake City. As I advance, England recedes, and the
chances are the next mail will carry no notes of
American Travel from the Far West, unless Mr.
Pullman's special private Car is so well hung, and
the Pacific Road is so well laid, as to permit in-
telligible writing in it.

CHAPTER VII.

CHICAGO.

Writing in the train is impossible unless one holds the paper with one hand and the pen in the other, so that the process is slow and irksome; however, in passing over a Prairie some 500 miles in length, writing or reading is a resource one gladly avails oneself of, and I will do my best to proceed with my notes. Having crossed the Missouri at Omaha, we are now in the " Far West," on the Union Pacific Line, traversing the boundless Plains or Prairies of Nebraska.

I must, however, go back to Chicago, for to pass over that city of such solid, yet such mushroom growth, would be an unpardonable omission. Chicago is the capital of the West, and is estimated to number no less than 460,000 inhabitants; but yesterday it had no existence—in 1830 it had but 12 houses and 100 inhabitants; 34 years ago it had only 7,580 ; 27 years since 28,269, since which it has advanced with giant strides, and especially since the fire of 1871, when we all remember that nearly the whole city was burnt to the ground—strange to say, almost no trace of that fire can now be seen; the houses are not only solid but princely; in fact, I scarcely know to what to compare them, except to the great Manchester warehouses or to some of the costly new ranges of offices in the City. I asked a friend who was kind enough to lionise me, how men who had lost their all had contrived to find money to build such expensive blocks ? He explained, first, that the sums received for insurances were very large, and next, that many mortgages existed prior to the fire, and that the mortgagors were compelled to advance money to rebuild in order to avail themselves of the value of the sites.

Be that as it may, the city has been completely rebuilt, and is now one of the finest in the Union. Magnificent Churches abound—there are upwards of 200 in Chicago—31 Roman Catholic, 26 Baptists, 26 Presbyterian, 27 Methodist, 19 Episcopal, 10 Congregational, 5 Jewish, and the balance various. Michigan Avenue is remarkable for the number of fine Churches which line its broad roadway, and I must again compliment their architects on their originality, and fine architecture generally, although, of course, there is also much of a debased character : in the main they are solid and costly structures, in good taste, and built in no niggardly spirit. Handsome villas abound here as elsewhere, and give evidence of wealth and the yearning for the comforts of home life inherent in our race.

The sights of Chicago are its Grain Elevators and Stock Yards ; the former are lofty warehouses for the storage of grain and for its shipment. The cars containing the grain are run in on the basement, two men then enter, each with a large shovel, say three or four feet wide, to which a rope connected with the machinery is attached. This rope is alternately drawn in and slackened out. The man draws the shovel inward as the rope slackens, and then, after plunging it deep into the grain, guides it to the side door, while the rope tightens : in this way masses of grain are shot out of the car with but little manual labour. From the car it falls into hoppers, from whence an endless belt with buckets lifts it to the top of the warehouse, about 160 feet high. It is then discharged into a hopper weighing machine, from whence it falls into other hoppers, where it remains till wanted for shipment. When required the grain is again lifted and passed through the hopper-weighers, from whence it is run by long spouts into the ships. The process is carried on almost entirely by mechanical power, the men only superintending the working of the machinery. Some idea of the size of the great grain warehouses may be gathered from the fact that the Elevator I went over could store fifteen hundred thousand bushels, and that the machinery was set in motion by a 300 h. p. engine.

The report of the Board of Trade on the transactions of Chicago in 1876 is before me, and I see from it that 87,241,306 bushels of Flour and Grain passed through Chicago in that year, value 57,100,000 dollars ; Live Stock, 57,500,000 dollars ; Products of Cattle and Hogs, 68,200,000 dollars ; Dairy Produce, 8,200,000 dollars ; Wool and Hides, 25,700,000 dollars ; Wines and Spirits, 8,500,000 dollars ; Sundries, 6,250,000 dollars ; Total, 231,450,000 dollars ; or about £46,290,000.

It will be seen how important the trade in the " Products of Cattle and Hogs" is, being nearly Fourteen Millions sterling. In 1875-6 no less than 2,320,846 Hogs were slaughtered at Chicago, and 1,096,725 head of Cattle passed through its markets.

The Hog Products " Manufacture" is one of the great sights of Chicago. The Stock Yards are situated about five miles outside the City to the south. A kind friend drove me out in his light four-wheel " buggy," with his " Trotter," which can do its mile in three minutes. The morning, 7 a.m., was lovely, as usual in this delicious climate. Our road lay through the Michigan Avenue to which I have already alluded, and then through partially-built suburbs over very rough roads, none at all in some places, but the spider-like buggy negotiated the deepest depressions and highest banks like a prac-tised hunter, and we soon found ourselves approaching an immense Hotel devoted exclusively to drovers and stock dealers. Passing it we entered the cattle pens, strong post and rail enclosures, each of some acres in extent. I was told that the yards extend over some hundreds of acres.

I saw one prime lot of shorthorns. Next to them a lot of Texans, very inferior ; but in truth I had not time to take stock of the yards, and, moreover, the business is not at this moment very active. They were not killing, but I am told that the process is thus conducted : They drive the animals

N

into a long passage; a man walks on a platform above them with a small breech-loading rifle and shoots them behind the head—a single shot disposes of each in the most painless way.

I visited the Hog Product Manufactory, which, though not savory, is well worthy of a short description. The hogs are slaughtered methodically and mercifully, but with extraordinary rapidity. They are driven to the top of a two-storied building, where a pen is provided capable of holding 20 or 30 hogs; in this a man stands with a short iron chain shackle, which he fastens to the right hind leg of the pig, and then attaches it to a rope working round a pulley. Another man stands on a stage above, and throws the pully into gear, when up goes poor piggy, and almost before he can squeal he finds himself head down and heels up. The man then shifts the shackle on to a hook attached to a " traveller" running on a rail, and pushes piggy a few feet on to the butcher who stands below with his knife level with the beast's throat. A scientific thrust and cut, and poor piggy is good pork. He is then pushed on, giving a few convulsive struggles, until he is brought up by the carcase of his predecessor. Half-a-dozen or a dozen carcases are allowed to collect on the travelling railroad to insure the first being quite dead. It is then lowered into a long tank of boiling water, along which a row of men stand, who push the carcases slowly forward. At the end, a huge bent pronged fork lies in the bottom of the tank; this is lifted by machinery, and whips the carcase out by the rapid

action of a crank, landing it on a slightly inclined
table, on each side of which a row of men stand,
naked to the waist, and armed with scrapers. They
remove the hair more and more completely as the
carcase advances, until in an incredibly short time
after death it presents the appearance we see in a
butcher's shop.

After leaving the table it is dressed, the offal
being carefully separated for its various uses ; the head
and feet are cut off, and the carcase is pushed away
on long lines of " travellers" to the cooling department,
where it hangs for several hours, and is then trammed
into the ice chamber, where it is kept 48 hours, after
which it is cut up to suit the markets, into Wilt-
shire, Staffordshire, Stretford, Yorkshire, Birmingham, and Irish sides, as well as into pieces of solid
fat for the French market—hams and other forms of
bacon.

The offal is boiled into lard and grease, and the
residue pressed for manure. The hocks and
tongues are specially prepared ; in fact, nothing is
wasted. A facetious friend of ours summed it up by
saying that piggy trotted in at one end, and came
out at the other as bacon, ham, sausage, hair-brush,
and saddle, nothing but his squeal being wasted, and
that before long the telephone would probably utilise
that also.

In 1849-50 there were 1,652,220 hogs packed, while
last year there were 4,887,999 disposed of in the
Mississippi Valley. A considerable proportion of the
product is exported to Europe, and yet I am not

aware that our markets have been ruinously affected by this immense addition.

The question arises, how far the importation of dead meat—beef and mutton—and live stock will affect prices with us? I am sorry to say that my visit to Chicago has not enlightened me as much as I expected. I met three of the most extensive dealers in " Produce" at dinner, and discussed the question fully with them. They had not interested themselves about it, their business being " hog products;" but to my surprise they seemed to believe rather in canned meat than in live stock or dead meat on the refrigerator system. I disagree with them because canned meat is not popular with us. They seem to think that live stock should be sent to the ports and there slaughtered, but they said that the loss on the stock by this system was 20 per cent. I know that good judges are much divided between the two systems. My own impression is in favour of dead meat. The trade is as yet in its infancy, and has not hardened into a solid business.

I must be content to do my best, from the information I possess, to state the present condition of this most important and interesting question, but I cannot pretend to exhaust the subject, and I beg that my statements may be accepted with all reserve as most imperfect.

The trade began at New York in October, 1875, with a shipment of 24,340lbs.; it steadily increased, till in April, 1876, it reached 1,193,233lbs.; in September, 1876, it was 2,047,217lbs.; and in December, 3,624,390lbs. ; in March, 1877, it reached to 5,797,817lbs. I have not been able to obtain accurate statistics of later date, but I am told that it has much diminished since, owing to the rise in the price of cattle on this side, and to the want of proper arrangements for its reception and storage on our side. Many of the refrigerator boxes are now being used for cheese and butter.

The vessels leaving New York fitted with refrigerators are—five of the Guion Line with an aggregate measurement used for meat, ice, and machinery connected with it of 4,030 tons ; five steamers of the White Star Line, 1,523 tons ; four Inman, 1,374 tons ; two Anchor Line, 340 tons ; two Cunarders, 320 tons ; one State Line, 170 tons ; total measurement tonnage devoted to this trade out of New York, 7,757.

From Philadelphia there were shipped in 1876 and 1877, 4,677,560lbs. ; and from Boston, 2,387,040lbs. When I was at Boston a contract was being negotiated with the Cunard Company for a considerable quantity, and they were contemplating fitting several of their ships with refrigerators.

It is said that the early shipments were profitable, but that the more recent have not been so. From various good sources I learnt that one penny per pound will cover railway carriage, freight and charges, from Chicago to Liverpool. What is the first cost ? I have before me the tabular statement published by the Board of Trade of the prices at Chicago during 1876, and under the heading, "Cattle, good to

choice," I find that the range of price for quality was
as much as from 3 dollars 75 cents. to 6 dollars 20
cents. per 100lbs., or from 15s. to 24s. 10d., while on
another occasion I find a variation for quality of only
50 cents., or 2s. per 100lbs. The average of the
year 1876 for " Good " is 4 dollars 50 cents., and
" Choice " 5 dollars 31 cents. equal to from 16s. 2½d.
to 20s. 3d. per 100lb., or say roughly 2d. to 2½d. per
lb. Now this is for the beast as it stands; into the
mysteries of the trade I had better not attempt
to enter, for I know nothing about them. How
much horn, hoof, and hide, bring to the credit, and
offal and bone to the debit, I know not; but
there are many who know to an ounce what 2d.
to 2½d. per lb. gross would equal in best and second
cuts. I have a general idea that meat could be
delivered in England at about 6d. per lb., or at most
7d. per lb., and I am old enough to remember meat
at that price with us.

Now we come to the question of supplies, and how
far increased demand will cause prices to advance?
I am at this moment writing on the western side
of the Rocky Mountains, about 30 miles as the crow
flies from Salt Lake City and 1,400 from Chicago;
I have just passed a train laden with cattle evidently for that market. In that 1,400 miles I have
traversed some 700 miles of the finest corn growing
country, and probably about 400 miles of what I am
told is the finest grazing country possible, in passing
over the vast Prairies of Nebraska and Wyoming,
where but a short time ago countless herds of Buffalo

roamed, animals of kindred race and wants. I was told two days ago by Mr. Dillon, President of the Union Pacific Railway, and himself interested in a herd of 12,000 head, that cattle live out all the winter and get fat on the Prairie grass. What the exact limits of this great grazing country are, I know not, but the United States extend about 1,250 miles from North to South at this point, and I know that there are no finer lands than those of Texas on the Southern and Dakota on the Northern extremity of that wide range; here and there, it is probable, that there are barren districts, but in the main I believe the bulk of the immense area, represented by these figures, say roughly 1,250 miles from North to South, and 400 from East to West, or 500,000 square miles, is grazing land. Mr. Dillon said that when it is " filled up," *i.e.*, fully stocked, its produce would be enormous. They are now filling it up by buying Texan cows and crossing them with first-class short-horn bulls. At present one travels miles without seeing a herd.

What number of acres are required on the average for a beast, I suppose no one can say. My impression is that at present any great demand for meat of good quality would cause the price to rise, and I therefore think that this trade, like others, must be gradual in its growth, but that at and above a price of, say 7d. in England per lb., it is certain to flourish and extend.

I have chiefly alluded to the grazing lands, but for 700 miles west of Chicago I passed through the finest possible corn country, and I am told that the farmers are turning their attention more and more to stock feeding : this band of corn land is of great extent north and south. The inevitable conclusion is that in process of time, when herds have been created, the supply will be unlimited.

I am now in Salt Lake City, and I was told to-day that 20,000 head of cattle were sent from hence last year to Chicago, 1,500 miles, and that they realised satisfactory prices. My informant, the son of a Birmingham cattle drover, now one of the wealthiest men in Utah, sent 150 head a short while ago to Chicago, and realised about 2½d. per lb. gross. He tells me that the net varies from 60 per cent. to 50 per cent. of the gross weight according to the condition of the animal, and that the offal is equal to about ½d. per lb., so that 2½d. gross=5d., net less ½d.=4½d., to which add 1d. for freight and charges to Liverpool.

As a proof of the high quality of land here, he told me that he killed a four-year-old last year which made 1,400lbs. net and 250lbs. of rough tallow. From these facts it is plain that the District of Utah will also come in to supply the Chicago market. Utah is a country made up of steep mountains and fertile valleys ; cattle feed on the mountains in summer, and in winter in the valleys. The exact extent I cannot state, but it must be considerable.

I have not mentioned sheep, because I neither saw nor heard of any at Chicago or on my journey across the Prairie, except one flock which I saw in a valley near here. I am told that the mountains of Utah suit them well, and that there are about 150,000 head within the territory. The average clip of wool is about 5lbs., and it fetches about 12½d. per lb. My information as to meat goes no further. I must endeavour to perfect it at New York, where I hope to hear of the commercial results and prospects of this most important trade.

CHAPTER VIII.

I MUST now go back somewhat and journey over the long stretch of the Great Pacific Railway which I have traversed between Chicago and Salt Lake City, 1,500 miles. And first let me occupy a moment in describing the " car yacht" in which we embarked—Mr. Pullman's private car, quite new, and fitted with every luxury the heart of the most fastidious could desire. At the forward or train end, a kitchen; then a pantry; then a gentleman's lavatory; then two berths, seats during the day, and as good beds as I ever slept in at night; then a drawing-room, with an harmonium and cylinder writing desk, a square table drawing out to a sufficient length to dine ten, arm chairs, ordinary chairs, and a sofa; then a state-room, with large double bed, and a lavatory off it; and last, a saloon or observatory, with a sofa and arm chairs, plate-glass windows the full size of the sides and end, and a door opening on to the outside platform, capable of holding four chairs, and enclosed by an iron railing. As we are always at the end of the train, we sit on the platform for hours in this fine climate, and have an unbroken view of the scenery. The best messman was selected to cater for us, two black servants to wait on us (really I love these blackies, they are such quick, good-natured, excellent servants), and the best cook to cook for us. To talk of the hardships of a journey under such circumstances would be an ungrateful romance. In fact, we all arrived at the end of our four days and three nights as fresh as when we started.

Our first day's journey lay through the rich plains of Illinois, a really fertile farming country—large corn fields thick with high maize, fine rich clover fields, regular fences and some hedges, substantial farm-buildings, and herds of good cattle. Just as night came on we crossed the great Mississippi, even here a mighty river. We stood on our platform as we crossed it, and watched the distant lights of Burlington mirrored in its glassy waters, and marking its great breadth.

Dinner and a rubber brought the first day of car life to a close; a good night's rest, and the waking hour just in the early twilight succeeded by as lovely a sunrise as I ever saw. Long stratus-clouds in the east, tinged first with that peculiar transparent green, which neither artist can imitate nor pen describe, only to be seen in the clearest and purest atmospheres, then with the most glowing ruby, reflected on to a mass of nimbus high in the western sky, which was soon to be converted into delicate salmon hues, all rapidly to fade into the hard tints of every-day skies. This was my waking vision, as I raised the heavy curtain of my berth and gazed on the early dawn. while as far as the eye could reach the earth was clothed in an abundant harvest of Indian Corn.

We are now in Iowa, not so trim and finished in its farming as Illinois, but still a splendidly rich district. I am told that the wheat-growing lands lie north and south; we passed but few—all Indian corn. The eye soon wearies of tall maize fields. The dark heavy blind is drawn down, and a couple of hours' doze, with now and then a peep at the country, ensue.

Breakfast, and then the Missouri is reached—the dirtiest, ugliest river I ever saw in my life. Its valley is a wide dreary mud flat, with which it plays all kinds of tricks—altering its course for miles at a bound; Council Bluffs, which a few years ago were on its banks, are now three miles away. It is crossed by a splendid light iron bridge, of nine spans, 250 feet each. Two were carried away by a cyclone and spate last year. The railway people will find they have a tough job to keep this reckless river in order. The water looks like liquid mud—worse than the Severn at Gloucester.

We reached Omaha, on the banks of the Missouri, at 10 a.m. on Sunday; and as the train stayed there some hours, we went to a nice little Episcopal Church, somewhat too elevated for me. However, they are free agents here, and are subjected to no tyranny, nor need any congregation allow practices of which they do not approve. On our way we passed a Church which was being moved bodily to another part of the town. Much of the wonder ceases when we remember that these structures are of wood, and naturally hold together like a gigantic box.

Omaha is the last city of the West. After you pass it you are in the " Far West"—in the State of Nebraska. The " City" has rather a weird, disorderly look—wide would-be streets, frame houses out of all proportion to their grand position, avenues not grown up, roads not made ; but it is to be, and I daresay will be, a great place. It has an Episcopal Church, Bishop, and University.

Back from Church, and "all aboard ;" but this time our car was not the last of the train. Behind it was the official car of the directors of the Union Pacific Railroad, and in it Mr. Dillon (the President of the line) and Mr. Jay Gould (a Director, well-known in the railway world). Mr. Dillon was one of the original projectors of this great undertaking, and drove the last spike, made of iron, silver, and gold, when the Central Pacific, approaching from the West, met the Union Pacific, coming from the East, at a point seven miles beyond Ogden, near Salt Lake City. The spike bears a suitable inscription, and Mr. Dillon has it now, for, as he told me, " the hole was bored large enough, and he took care not to hit it too hard, so that he soon had it out again." These gentlemen gave us most interesting information as we went along, much of which I have already embodied.

Our track lay over a flat low-lying country—the valley of the Platte. In the distance, say ten miles off, were low hills, and alongside the old Mormon track across the Desert to the Promised Land. The railway follows it almost exactly, often within a dozen feet, for 1,000 miles, over Prairie and Desert, until the Valley of the Salt Lake is at last reached. All along we saw their old " ranches," or resting-places, and I thought as I looked at the track with what varied emotions of joy and sorrow, hope and fear, many weary souls must have toiled along in their tilted waggons, leaving much that was dear for ever behind, and journeying on to the unknown future.

In the Platte Valley there are patches of corn (maize), but the ground is mostly covered with a coarse rank grass, as high as the back of a calf I saw feeding in it. I believe all this is capable of growing corn.

Night came on, and we were still running through the same kind of country. At break of day the high coarse grass had given place to tufty short prairie grass, which I was told afforded much fine feed. Hour after hour the same country : upland downs rising into round-topped hills stretching away as far as the eye could reach. These were the Buffalo Plains of old, and here and there we saw the bleaching bones and skulls of those killed and left to rot by wasteful white men. Twice we saw a herd of antelopes, and a few little prairie dogs sitting on their tails or scampering into their holes.

In the middle of the day we approached Cheyenne, a place of a few thousand inhabitants, whence a branch Railroad leads to Denver City, in Colorado.

Up to that point from Omaha the gradient had been
fifteen feet to the mile against us, but from here on
to Sherman Station it is frequently 1 in 120. We
gradually rose until we reached a granite plateau,
with characteristic " Tors," like the Cornish, protruding through the surface. To the south-west were the
high ranges of Colorado about Denver, fine outlines
with snow in their northern hollows. At length,
about 3 p.m., we reached Sherman Station, 8,300 feet
above the sea level, the summit of the Rocky
Mountains—the Great Divide of America, from which
to the West the waters flow by the Rio Colorado to
the Pacific, while to the East they flow to the
Atlantic. This is the highest point on the Pacific
Railway, and I was glad to find that the backbone
of America was granite and porphyry, with an outburst of serpentine, like the old Lizard.

From Sherman we ran rapidly down about 2,000
feet to the plateau leading to the Warsatch range,
and when night closed in we were still in prairie
country. I was told we were to pass coal mines at
5 a.m., at a place called " Rock Springs," and I left
orders to be called. Bleak and bitter was the morning, and dreary was the outlook—a perfect desert.
Sand and tufts of a kind of heath-sedge, with
white alkaline eflorescence covering every spot where
water had been. The collieries puzzled me at first,
as I saw neither shaft nor level. At last I discovered in a little stream the crop of a huge vein,
about thirty or forty feet thick ; and I saw that they
were driving down slants upon it. The coal is black,

cubical, and full of gas; but I believe it must be "lignite," or brown coal, and I think it is in the Oolite formation, just as I once saw coal occur in the Maremma Tuscana, in Italy. The rocks have all the character of that formation.

Mr. Jay Gould told me that at one place they have two beds of 50 feet thick each, and two of 25 feet; while at another they bored 1,100 feet for water, and cut through a number of viens, the least of which was 8 feet thick. The discovery is a great godsend to this railway and to the country. It has reduced the cost of coal on this line from 16s. to 5s. per ton.

We ran down the dreary and desolate valley of the Green River, which is in reality the upper waters of the Colorado, and then ascended to the summit of the Warsatch range, 7,800 feet, through a barren and uninteresting country. After passing the summit we rapidly descended through Echo Canyon and Weber Canyon to the great Salt Lake Valley. These canyons are fine mountain gorges, overhung first by beetling precipices of red sandstone conglomerate, then by Silurian and older Eozoic rocks, presenting much the same features as the gorges of the Alps and Apennines, wanting, however, the snowclad serrated outlines of the Oberland or Chamouni —fine passes, but I have seen many similar and some finer. The light lasted us through them, but night fell before we reached the City of the Salt Lake.

Salt Lake City, more properly the Mormon community, deserve more than passing notice. With

the Mormon religion I have nothing to do. I am
wholly unacquainted with their doctrines, and if I
knew them thoroughly I should have no wish to set
myself up as my brother's judge. They call themselves Christians, and say they have received certain
recent revelations. We need hardly discuss the probability of recent revelations or recent miracles. Nor
need I enter on any argument as to polygamy, which
they believe to be permissible, as the Patriarchs of
old and the nations of the East, but which we believe
to be wrong. I shall speak of them as a Community
only, and state what I saw.

The territory of Utah is almost entirely peopled
by Mormons, of whom there are estimated to be
140,000. In Salt Lake City there are about 25,000
inhabitants, of whom, I was told, 20,000 are Mormon. The Gentile, *i.e.*, non-Mormon, population at
Salt Lake City are chiefly connected with mining
and trade. The Mormon population are mostly agricultural, although there are many men of business
among them who have made large fortunes, and have
taken a leading part in the development of their
country by constructing railways throughout it, as
far as their means would permit.

They produce within their own territory almost
everything they require ; they export cattle and all
kinds of agricultural produce, for their land has been
made very fertile by their industry. It is not here
as in Illinois or Dakotta, to plough and sow the
deep, rich soil, and reap an abundant harvest with
but little forethought or labour ; here nothing can

P

be done without irrigation ; water has to be brought from the valleys which debouche on the plains, and then the naturally good soil and fine climate yield abundantly. It is almost safe to say that no cereal, fruit, or flower refuses to flourish in Utah. I saw wheat, barley, oats and maize, sugar cane, clover and lucerne in great abundance, the latter yielding three crops. Peaches, on standard trees, as large and good as our English peaches, magnificent pears, equal to the best that Jersey or France can produce, apples, and black Hambro' grapes ripe in the open air ; the muscat grape will not ripen completely ; roses, geraniums, verbenas, and every kind of flower we prize ; in fact, the climate is excellent, and being upwards of 4,000 feet above the sea, the district is very healthy. The mulberry flourishes, and they are commencing to cultivate it for the production of silk. There is a look of home and comfort about the cottages, which are built of brick, stone, or "adobe" (sundried brick), and are surrounded by groves of trees. In fact, planting has been one of the distinctive features of Mormon cultivation.

The City of Salt Lake occupies a very commanding position on the Eastern side of the valley, which at this point is from 15 to 20 miles wide. It stands on gradually rising ground, about 150 feet above the level of the Lake, at the foot of a range of mountains, which attain an elevation of 6,000 to 8,000 feet above the plain, and 10,000 to 12,000 above the sea, with fine serrated outlines, intersected by deep lateral gorges, here called "Canyons," at the head of

one of which the famous mines of this district, the
Flagstaff, Emma, &c., are situated. Clear cold
mountain torrents of pure water, issue from these
Canyons and irrigate the thirsty alkali-covered plain,
thus supplying the inhabitants with the necessaries
of life in plentiful abundance.

With the exception of the Tabernacle there are
no buildings worthy of note in Salt Lake City. But
the Tabernacle is a structure, the like of which I
have never seen before. I can compare it only to
a Dutch built craft, bottom up, no keel, and
rounded stem and stern. It consists of a wooden
shingle roof, with rather a graceful curve, and a
rounded "hip" at both ends. It is said to seat
12,000 people, and has had 15,000 within its
capacious borders. Yet its acoustic properties are so
wonderfully good that a person speaking, without any
special effort, can be heard from one end to the other.

The whole character of the building may be said
to turn upon the roof, the principals of which spring
from solid stone pillars ; they are formed of nine planks
two inches thick and three feet wide, bolted together
and the joints broken, or alternated. I think the arch
they form must be a semi. The interior is 233 feet
long and 133 feet wide; double rows of pillars on
each side support wide galleries. The floor of the
nave is thus arranged : For one third of its length
it is flat, and then rises rapidly like the stage of a
theatre. This rise, and the shape of the roof, no
doubt are the chief causes of the good acoustic properties of the building.

P 2

The organ is the second largest in America. It was constructed by a local organ builder in the place it now occupies, and is made entirely of native timber. It contains 3,000 pipes, the largest 2 feet square and 65 feet high. Four men are required to blow it. One of the ladies of our party played various tunes upon it, ending with " God save the Queen," to which the Mormon gentlemen who accompanied us in no way objected.

The Temple, a Cathedral in size, is being built of finely-dressed white granite. It is about 30 or 40 feet high at present. They are working slowly at it as funds are forthcoming. They build entirely without scaffolding by means of a small portable engine inside, which works lofty cranes with jibs of such length and strength as to pick up the heaviest stones outside and deposit them on the walls. When finished the building will have two stories internally.

I was rather puzzled at their requiring a Tabernacle and a Temple, nor do I quite understand it yet. The explanation given me was that the Tabernacle is used for prayer, preaching, and assemblies of the people, while the Temple is devoted to the ordinances of the Church : baptisms, including baptism of the dead, sealing, i.e., marriages, &c. The baptism of the dead is performed by proxy, and admits the deceased person to the Church, which they have the option of joining in heaven if they like.

The President occupies the highest pulpit in the Tabernacle, under the organ ; below him sit the 12 apostles, and on each side the high priests and bishops. At the side of the organ there are seats for a large choir, the men on one side and women on the other.

On our arrival at Salt Lake City we called on the United States' Governor and also on the President *pro. tem.* of the Mormon community, Mr. John Taylor, who we found at the office of the Zion House, formerly President Young's residence. The office is a low library with a large skylight and gallery. Around the walls are portraits of celebrated members of the Mormon church, beginning with the founder of the sect, Joseph Smith, and his brother, who were murdered in Illinois when the people rose against the Mormons in 1846.

We were received with much the same formal politeness which we should have experienced on visiting the chief of any State Government, and our interview terminated in the usual manner.

We had letters of introduction to two of the most active men of business at Salt Lake ; one a director of the Union Pacific and of the Utah Southern Railroads, the other a highly successful merchant. They accompanied us by rail to the Salt Lake itself, 20 miles from the city—a beautiful spot, much frequented for bathing in summer. One of the ladies of our party bathed and found the water wonderfully buoyant, being in fact brine of such high specific gravity as to support the human body. It contains no less than 25 per cent. of salt, or I think about seven times as much salt as the sea. In former days, when the Mormons first arrived, it contained

33 per cent., but since then the water has risen ten feet, owing to a succession of wet seasons, and as the volume of salt has probably remained the same the considerable dilution above stated has resulted. This year the Lake has fallen two feet. I confess I should not feel comfortable if I were an owner of property in the Salt Lake Valley. I see no reason why a cycle of wet and cold season, by increasing the rainfall and reducing the evaporation, may not cause a very great rise of water. It is said that when the Mormons first encamped where their city now is, an old Indian told them that he had seen the water at that spot up to a horse's belly, although it is now 150 feet above the Lake. This I can scarcely credit, but there is the positive evidence of a raised beach, as marked as any I ever saw in the north of Norway, extending in every direction round the hill sides, that for a long series of years the level of the water was about 800 feet higher than at present, and that it then drained into the Colorado. This raised beach is indeed recognised by everyone as the former level of the water.

It does not seem probable that the lake was ever, except at some remote geological epoch, in communication with the sea, as it is 4,000 feet above it. There are salt springs near it, and its salt is probably due to the existence of a salt formation immediately adjacent. Indeed, rock salt is found not far off to the south.

The scenery of the Lake is very striking. To the west lofty hills bound it, while in its midst an island 20 miles long rises into the dignity of almost a mountain range, since it is some 2,000 feet high.

On the following day we made an early start for the famous " Emma Mine," which is situated at the head of the little Cottonwood Canyon, about 20 miles from Salt Lake City. The Southern Utah Railway passes the mouth of the Canyon at Sandy Station, 13 miles from Salt Lake City. At and near this station there are several smelting works. The ores of this district are mostly argentiferous galenas, and are therefore easily dealt with. One group of rich mines lie to the east of Sandy, and another in the range of mountains which form the western boundary of the valley. These latter mines are less rich in silver, but produce low grade lead ores in greater abundance. Narrow gauge (3ft.) railroads connect both mining districts with Sandy.

We chose the Eastern group because it included the " Emma" and " Flagstaff" mines, both well known in England. On reaching Sandy we embarked on board the narrow guage, not in a luxurious Pullman, but on a granite wagon without springs, A miner's chest formed my seat, while that of my *compagnon de voyage* was a keg, which might have been dynamite, but proved to be whisky.

The gradient was steep, but the little locomotive travelled up it like a mule, and we were not long in reaching the " raised beach," which my mountain aneroid gave as nearly 800ft. above Salt Lake City. Soon afterwards we entered the jaws of the Canyon, a crack in Silurian Rocks, highly inclined, and resting

against solid white granite, from which the stones for
the Temple are quarried.

We then again changed our train for small low
wagons, with three benches, and three on a bench, to
which two mules were harnessed to drag us up the
steep gradient. The first mile lay through a fine
gorge, which indeed continued to the end, but the
remainder of the railroad was covered by snow sheds,
and except glimpsewise, here and there, it was impossible to see anything, whilst the dust rose in clouds.
At the end of about an hour and a half we
emerged from our elongated imprisonment, and found
ourselves at the head of the gorge, and in presence of
the great " Emma Mine," marked, alas, only by a few
tumble-down wooden sheds on a very small scale,
presenting no external appearance of much outlay.

We toiled up the step hill to the mine itself, and
my aneroid marked a trifle under 8,900ft. above the
sea. On the " floor" was a small pile of nice ore,
compact galena and friable light green stuff, said to
be rich in silver, and possibly chloride. This was
being selected from the Halvens, and gave convinc-
ing proof of past carelessness and improvidence. The
Halvens appeared to me to be small compared to the
quantity of rich ore produced, which means that
little dead work had to be done, and that the ore
must have been but slightly mixed with waste.

I then went up to the mouth of the level, where
there were a couple of boilers, some winding gear, and
steampipes leading into the level, and little else in the
way of machinery. They have, I was told, 19 men

at work. I made no attempt to go underground, and am therefore unable to give any opinion of the Mine. I, however, fell in with a Cornishman, who gave me some information. How well founded, or how far I have remembered it accurately, I cannot say, but it may serve to give a general idea of the Mine.

The Mine was, no doubt, first discovered at the outcrop at grass, but they seem to have gone down the hill, and driven in 400ft. to cut the deposit. They then crossed it 270ft. in solid ore, and sank about the same depth upon it. To the east they had 60ft. in width, but to the west were cut off by compact limestone, in which they drove 70ft. without finding ore. Now I am not quite certain whether the man did not mean that the 270 driving and sinking were the same, as I fancy they went down on the slant. I was much hurried, and had only a hasty conversation, as I was forced to leave to catch the train, and I only fell in with the man ten minutes before I left. He told me that the bunch had quite cut out in the bottom, and that they had sunk 150ft. in dead ground. I do not vouch for the accuracy of this account, but give it only as I received it.

The mine is situated on the northern side of the gorge, halfway up the steep slope of a limestone escarpment, the beds dipping inwards, and therefore nearly north, so far as I could judge by the eye. I could see the crop of the limestone beds protruding through the herbage, and the run of mines exactly coincided with the strike of the beds. I therefore conclude that the occurrence of this ore is not in lodes or veins, but upon the line of one particular bed, which is probably subject to hollows or cavities (like those found in most limestone formations), which cavities have gradually become filled with ore from the subjacent strata by electrical action in the manner first suggested by Mr. Fox, of Falmouth, whose explanation of the formation of metallic deposits is the only one which has ever satisfied my mind, or which has appeared to me to square with almost all metallic " occurrences " (I use this word because we have none which applies as the German word " Vorkommen" does, and the sooner we fit one into our language the better) that I have seen, and I believe I have visited every mine of any magnitude in Europe, excepting Russian and Spanish mines. The great Monti Poni Mine in Sardinia certainly occurs in the same strata " Old Limestone," I suppose Laurentian, and between the beds, in irregular cavities, not interstratified but amorphous, just as the glimpse I had of the Little Cottonwood Canyon, leads me to believe the minerals occur there. Within sight, and probably within a mile or a mile and a half, and on the same run, are the following mines from the west to east :—The Flagstaff, South Star and Titus, Alta Consola, North Star, Highland Chief, Emma, Lavinia, and Bute. Over the hill, I was told, came the Antelope, Prince of Wales, Richard and Thersea, Reed and Benson, and Kate Hayes.

Deep below, in the basin-shaped amphitheatre at the head of the gorge, is the little mining village of

Alta; on the opposite hillside I saw other workings, but I did not visit them. This Canyon is producing about 100 tons daily of silver lead ore. Limestone mines, although often very rich for a time, are always bunchy and uncertain.

I was told that the history of the "Emma" is the following in a few words: It was discovered by a poor miner, who had resolved that if he was ever offered 100,000 dollars, *i.e.*, £20,000, for any discovery, he would sell it. He was offered 110,000 dollars for the "Emma" by a Mr. Hussey, a banker at Salt Lake City. and he sold it; it was put on the New York market for 1,500,000 dollars (£300,000), and transferred to the English market at £1,000,000 sterling. The details can be filled in from the records of the Court of Chancery and other courts in England and America; the moral can be drawn by anyone.

The talk of the place is that there is plenty of ore still to be got out of the mine, but when I asked those who said so if they had been underground and spoke of their own knowledge, they admitted that they had not, and did not know more about it than hearsay. A mine that has once been rich may be rich again; a cave narrows and widens and narrows again, and I look upon these limestone occurrences of ore in the same light. The old miner I talked to and who knew the mine well, denied that the timbering was bad and caused the mine to run together, and I confess I fancy he was correct, for I should greatly suspect the truth of that story. I

have dwelt on this Emma mine, because so many
in England are, or were, interested in it, and because, perhaps, mine is the only practised and
thoroughly disinterested eye that has ever looked at
it, short and cursory as my glance was.

We again seated ourselves on our little *chars-a-
bancs*, but this time "Dixey," the old mule, was
lashed on behind, and away we went down the
incline at a pace which tried even my nerves. I
believe we sometimes went 20 miles an hour, or
more, through the narrow snow sheds, and round
curves of unknown radius; in fact, we cleared the
eight miles in 40 minutes. Once the points were
wrong and we came to a dead halt, much to the injury
of my shins, which were the only things damaged,
most fortunately. The gradient is steep enough to
work self-acting inclines if the road were somewhat
straightened, and the stuff might then be got down
for a quarter of the cost; as it is, a mule can only
haul back empties equal to the conveyance of 2½ tons
in the other direction.

CHAPTER IX.

MORMONISM.

BEFORE leaving Mormondom perhaps I shall be expected to say a word or two about Polygamy, dis-
tasteful as the subject may be. I have no statistics
to record. I do not know how many Mormons have
more than one wife, or how many have any given
number. Brigham Young. is said to have had 19
when he died; three or four lived in the " Zion
House," and three or four more in the large house
adjoining—the " balance," as an American would
say, lived here and there throughout the town. I
was shown some of their houses. Sixty children were
named in his will, and he left each about 20,000
dollars or £4,000. He is supposed to have died
worth £400,000. He made £150,000 at one stroke
by sub-letting his Union Pacific Railway contracts.

A Mormon gentleman, who was exceedingly civil
to us and introduced us to his family, has now only
one wife, his other having died some six years ago.
He has ten sons, all of whom he is bringing up to
different occupations, and two daughters, as lady-like
and well educated as English young ladies. His
house is large and well furnished ; he has his fancy
farm of 300 acres, and a herd of 50 well-bred shorthorns, eight or ten miles by rail from the City, and

some 50 miles south a stock farm of 3,000 head. I presume he is not less well off than Brigham Young.

In Mormon society there is every grade—from those I have named to the pauper. Polygamy was economical, but it is now costly. In former days labour was scarce, and the women and their children worked and were profitable. To some extent that is still so among the poorest, but the rich find that their wives and daughters want fine clothes, and that the larger the family the more it costs.

The Mormon young ladies will not marry men who cannot afford to dress them as well as their neighbours, and the result is that many are not married at all, and many try to avoid involving themselves in Polygamous connections. A well-informed person said to me that the expensive dress of the present day had given a serious blow to Polygamy. I was told that in some cases wives live together in perfect harmony, while in others they require separate establishments.

The death of Brigham Young, who undoubtedly was a man of great mental capacity, puts Mormonism on its trial. They think it will strengthen them, as their organization and self-government are complete. Outsiders say that they must break up ; upon that I can express no decided opinion, but I incline to the former view.

The Mormon policy is to spread abroad, and occupy as much of the territory as they can. Each Mormon is expected to contribute one-tenth of his income, in kind, as " Tithing," and the money so raised amounts

to a very large sum : I think I was told fully
£100,000 per annum. This sum is used for the
purposes of the Church, but largely to promote im-
migration. They assist about 3,000 persons annually
to emigrate from Europe, paying all expenses, which
I believe are afterwards gradually repaid.

After our visit to the Mining District, we proceeded to join the main Pacific Railway route again
at Ogden, a distance of 36 miles from Salt Lake
City. Ogden is a Mormon town of considerable size,
in appearance very much like Salt Lake City, and
from its position at the junction of the arterial line
running South through Utah with the main line of
the Pacific Railway, I think it must become a place
of great importance.

We were detained for an hour at Ogden, where the
two Pacific Companies meet, and where passengers
dine, luggage is checked, and the train made up for
the 48 hours' run to San Francisco. It was pitch
dark before we moved off for our final journey to the
Pacific. The early portion of our route lay over a
most uninteresting country : first along the northern
end of Salt Lake, where some cultivated lands exist
for about 50 miles, and then through an absolute
desert, about 60 miles square, after passing which
the country is said to be suitable for cultivation.

I confess that when I awoke at daylight, I suppose
some 200 miles from Ogden, the prospect was not an
inviting one, although I saw a few cattle here and
there. We were passing through a wide valley, with
a low range of hills on each side, and a small stream

running between thick willow beds in the bottom. The land was covered with sage-brush. Nothing appears to grow between the bushes on the light sandy soil.

I am writing in the train, and we are now some 90 miles further on our journey. During these 90 or 100 miles, to my eye, there has been but little change in the vegetation. We are passing a long train laden with tea. San Francisco supplies all America with tea, and I hear tea for England is beginning to take this route. It feels like getting on towards China ! !

We are still traversing a wide plain covered with the bunchy low growing heath-like plant called sage brush, each bunch separated from its neighbour by a foot or a yard of light sandy soil, upon which I can detect absolutely no vegetation. I can see perhaps 30 miles in one direction and 10 in the other, but not a living thing can I discern—fine ranges of hills from 1,000 to 2,000 feet high, of varied outline and configuration and brown hue, bound the plain on all sides, but I cannot detect any valley.

I wrote the above half an hour ago, and we have now crossed the plain and closed with the Humboldt River, along the banks of which are herds of cattle and droves of horses. It is evidently a question of "water," just as it is in Egypt, where the construction of the Sweetwater Canal converted a desert tract into rich land.

But to return. At 8 a.m., after leaving Ogden the night before, we reached "Elko," a railway station, whence the important mining district of Cope draws its supplies. Between Elko and Palisade (so spelt) we passed through two fine Canyons or Gorges, regular mountain passes, through which the Humboldt River finds its way, not to the sea, but to the Lake of the same name, in which, and the Lake Carson close by it disappears either by evaporation or by sinking into a subterranean channel.

The first Canyon has nothing of special interest, but the second is very striking throughout its course of 12 miles. Igneous action is frequently apparent in the rocks through which the Pass winds. They seemed to me to be metamorphic rocks changed to deep red and purple by igneous action, and I also saw actual eruptive rocks. The hills rise about a thousand feet above the line, now in isolated rugged masses, now in solid perpendicular walls, very properly called " The Palisades."

Two hideously ugly Indian squaws are looking in at the window, as I write, for we are now halting at a station, and I will be revenged by describing them. They have flat, broad, ugly, copper coloured faces,—in fact deeper brown than copper ; they look as if they had been left on a bed when babies and accidentally sat upon, so flat and broad are their faces ; their hair is raven black, coarse as horse hair, and hangs over their shoulders and back without an attempt at arrangement or ornament, the " Capilli intonsi" of old Horace. They are dressed in dirty cotton shirts, one has a red, the other a brown, jacket; their feet are protected by a sort of mocassin of rough hide,

R

through which in one case the toes protrude.   At a station a few miles back we watched five of these ugly types of humanity squatted in a circle on their heels and in other less graceful attitudes, playing cards—dirty and coarse looking to the last degree. One had her cheeks, forehead and chin painted deep vermillion ; five· of their lords and masters also sat round at a little distance and gambled with cards for black pebble markers, which had a cash value—for each had his small heap of silver also.   What the game was I do not know, but they were expert at it and kept their hands hidden under their jackets. One of these men had his face painted vermillion like the woman.

The men wear their hair long ; they have round black straw hats with wide bands and narrow brims, loose jackets and light trowsers.   I fancy they took their costume from the Mexicans, for we are now in Nevada Territory, which once belonged to Mexico. The station at which we saw these people was " Battle Mountain," near which a bloody battle was fought in early emigrant days, by which the power of the Shoshone tribe was broken.   Even while the railway was making, an encounter took place in this neighbourhood.   Now the Indians beg rather than steal. All is quiet ; and at the same station I saw the parts of a horizontal steam engine awaiting transport to one of the rich mines with which this country abounds.

Palisade Station is the point of departure for the districts of Mineral Hill, Treasure City, Eureka,

Spring Valley, Secret Canyon, Grantsville, &c.
These lie 30 to 150 miles south of the rail, while to
north lie Cope, Bull Run, Bruno, &c. "Eureka
Consols" has been a good mine for some years.

The dust along this part of the line is very
disagreeable. What between it and the hot dry air
I require no blotting paper when I turn over a leaf.
The temperature has been 75deg. in the shade all
day, at an elevation of between 4,000ft. and 5,000ft.

Four o'clock p.m. : We are still passing through
the same description of country,—sage-brush plains
and lofty mountains rising 2,000ft. or 3,000ft. above
them.

As the shades of evening lengthened, and the
waning sun cast a long line of gold across the distant
plain through a narrow gorge in the mountain range
beneath which it was sinking, we approached the
small Station of Humboldt, half way between Ogden
and San Francisco. There was an inexpressible
charm and relief about that place, for it was a true
oasis in the great Desert through which we had been
passing with such wearied senses ; yet it was in the
midst of the sage-brush Desert. There were shady
acacia and other trees, the greenest grass, maize, a
fruit orchard, a small pond with a mandarin duck
and white-fronted geese. All the fertility was due
to water brought from adjacent hills. The story is
the same here as in Egypt,—give it water, and the
Desert will bear abundantly.

Night came on, and we were still on the Desert,
but soon to leave it, and to climb the eastern slope

R 2

of the Sierra Nevada. It is dark now soon after
six. We therefore dined early, and resolved to
avail ourselves of every atom of daylight to enjoy
the grandeur of the scenery. I awoke at four,
and found we were toiling up the steep ascent
under long lines of continuous snow sheds. The
engine panted with a sterterous and oppressed
breathing : that harsh metallic sound which indicates
the labouring lung and the overtaxed piston alike.
I could see the stars and tall pine trees through the
cracks of the boarding. Soon we stopped at the
summit of the Sierra Nevada, 7,017ft. above the
sea ; distant from San Francisco, 245 miles.

Then we began to run merrily down the western
slope to the Pacific. I was soon on the rear platform
of the car, but we were passing under an unbroken
line of snow sheds, of which there are 45 miles,
covering the entire width of the Railway in its
passage through the snow line. The snow sometimes
lies 16ft. to 20ft. deep in this portion of the line.

I could see pines and the outlines of hilltops
through the cracks in the boarding ; once or twice a
few planks were wanting, and I caught sight of lovely
upland mountain scenery, deep ravines, clad with fine
old spruce and pine trees.

At last the endless sheds ended, and we were
rewarded by a grand view. We were winding round
the steep sides of a deep ravine, our engine almost
at right angles to us. Behind us were the blue
mountain tops which we had passed over, before us
ridge succeeding ridge, clad from foot to summit with

spruce and pine, not the puny trees we usually see, but grand giants of the primeval forest, many feet in diameter, straight as arrows, and carrying up their bulk high into the air; I dare not venture on guessing the height; as we rushed along I fancied that I recognised many of them as the specimen trees of our own Pinetum.

The train stopped at Blue Canyon Station, which is situated on an "Elvan course traversing Killas," as a Cornish man would say, that is a band of white porphyritic rock passing through clay slate. In our descent we passed one outburst of trap, and one of serpentine, with great masses of metamorphic rocks, exhibiting stronger evidences of igneous action than I have almost ever seen; in fact, this is a thoroughly igneous district.

We soon came in sight of American Canyon, so deep and precipitous as to be impassible, and then passing Alta, an upland village, we saw to our north the very extensive gold washings of Dutch Flat. In every direction launders, called here "flumes," constructed to carry water to the washings, cling to the hill sides, while more modern wrought-iron pipes traverse hill and dale without regard to level, bent on the same auriferous errand.

The gold diggings look like great white sheets spread on the green woodland sward, framed in by lofty pines, many of which are still standing. The little village of Dutch Flat, with its frame houses and white church, looks neat and homely. In decending the rapid incline, we passed several gold diggings, and soon reached the bend called " Cape Horn," the show-view of the line, where the train stops for five minutes on the brink of a precipice 1,200ft. deep, to enable the passengers to enjoy the scenery. All get out, stand on the giddy edge, and gaze at this fine gorge. We do ditto, and so does our cook, who takes the opportunity of our stoppage to get some chicken and mutton chops for breakfast out of the larder,—a very cleverly-arranged refrigerator under the car,—in doing this he placed his tin can too near the precipice, over which it rolled to the great amusement of the passengers. We heard it clattering down long afterwards, as it bounded from rock to rock.

A little further on, at Colfax Station, we took on board some splendid Californian grapes, bunches and berries which would take prizes at an English Horticultural Show; also some delicious pears, juicy and melting. We felt we were entering a Southern clime.

It was not until we reached Newcastle Station, 74 miles from the summit, that I saw any granite, and we had by that time descended some 6,000ft. In doing so we ran out of the pine forests with scattered oak, into a band of Ilex (evergreen oak) exactly like the growth of Italy. Indeed, the feeling of the air reminded me strongly of the sensation one experiences in descending the southern slopes of the Alps and entering Italian territory.

At 104 miles from the summit we arrived at Sacramento City, which we have just left, and are now passing over the rich but flat valley of the

Sacramento River, very nearly at the sea level, with
the thermometer at 90deg. in the shade. We stayed
but 20 minutes at Sacramento, during which we
walked about the town, and found it to be quite of
Spanish type—flat-topped houses, with wide veran-
dahs on each storey, covering the footways like
arcades ; all the stores or shops open to the street.

We have now 139 miles to San Francisco, and are
3,365 from New York, and, roughly, 6,500 from
home. I have not altered my watch since I left
England, and it is just eight hours out. If correct,
we are thus one-third round the world.

In crossing the Sierra Nevada, I saw no lofty
snow-capped mountains, and I believe that, near the
railway, there is nothing higher than 10,000ft. Those
who expect the Pacific route to delight them with
the lofty rugged outlines of the Swiss or even
Maritime Alps, will be disappointed. Whatever
there may be in other portions of this great mountain
range, there is no such scenery on the Pacific Railway,
fine though some of it undoubtedly is.

Perhaps most of my countrymen are as ignorant
as I was of the Physical Geography of this portion
of the American Continent ; in other words, of its
Section from east to west. They probably fancy,
as I did, that the Rocky Mountains on the east, and
the Sierra Nevada on the west, are one and the same
lofty mountain range, and that their summit is the
east and west watershed of this Continent, not being
aware that two very curious basins are interposed
which have no outlet to the sea. At Creston, on the

summit of the Rocky Mountains, we undoubtedly
cross the " Great Divide," for on the east the waters
flow to the Atlantic, while on the west they flow by
the Colorado River to the head of the Gulf of
California on the Pacific.   Creston is 7,100ft. above
the sea.   (The highest point crossed by the Pacific
Line is Sherman, 8,242ft., but the Head Waters of
the North Platte, which flow to the east, are west
of Sherman.)   From Creston we have a down grade
of 1,110ft. in 108 miles to Green River, which is
really the head water of the Rio Colorado, and thus
flows to the Pacific ; after which we rise to 7,835ft.
at Aspen, on the Wasatch Range, 92 miles to the
west.   After Aspen we descend to the Salt Lake
Basin, and at Ogden reach the level of only 4,301ft.
The Salt Lake Basin has no known outlet.   We
then ascend until we reach the summit of Cedar
Pass, at an elevation of 6,118ft. at Moore's Station,
305 miles from Aspen, after which there is a descent
for 311 miles to the Nevada Desert.   The drainage
of this Basin is represented by the rivers Humboldt
and Carson, both of which flow into Carson Lake, 20
to 25 miles long, and 10 wide, and are there lost.
What becomes of them no one knows.   Some say
there are sinks in the Lake, and some that evaporation takes off the surplus water.

It seemed to me that the Humboldt River was
smaller by far when we saw it on the plains not far
from Humboldt, than it was 100 miles nearer its
source.   It has a total course of 350 miles before
reaching Lake Humboldt, which is 35 miles long by

10 wide, and may cause much loss by evaporation. The elevation of Lake Carson is not given, but just beyond it Desert Station is said to be 4,017ft., and we have thus a fall of 2,101ft. in the Humboldt Basin.

From this we rise to the great backbone of the Sierra Nevada at Summit Station, 7,017ft. high, 3,000ft. above the Humboldt Basin, the total width of which from Cedar Pass to Summit Station is 427 miles.

We have thus (after passing the " Great Divide " at Creston) the Green River Basin, which has a breadth of 200 miles, and a depth of 1,100ft. ; after passing Aspen, the Salt Lake Basin, which has a breadth of 305 miles, and a depth of 3,534ft. ; and after passing Cedar Pass, the Humboldt Basin, which has a breadth of 427 miles and depth of 2,101ft. ; and four water-sheds, viz., Creston, Aspen, Cedar Pass, and Sierra Nevada Summit, in 932 miles, instead of one great Divide, as I had supposed.

While I have been working out these figures we have been crossing the great Sacramento Plain, fertile no doubt, but hot, dusty, almost treeless and uninteresting, brown and burnt up, with the thermometer at 90deg. in the shade on the 6th October.

As I knew that the Sacramento River flowed into the Harbour of San Francisco, I was not prepared for another minor Pass before we reached that city. After some hours on the plain, we entered a very lovely gorge in a mountain range, and following it, reached an elevation of 700ft. above the plain. The hills rise on each side in bold sweeping outlines,

s

brown and burnt by the hot sun, but relieved by
patches of "live oak" much like the Italian Ilex,
to an elevation, I should suppose, of 2,000ft. The
strata is much contorted, and, I think, is chiefly
composed of metamorphic rocks.

After running for some miles through this fine
gorge, called the "Alameda Canyon," we again enter
the plain, and turn north-west towards San Francisco, with the distant Sea Loch on our left, and the
mountain range through which we had just passed
on our right. The plain is highly cultivated, stubble
succeeding stubble, substantial homesteads, and large
flocks and herds; the houses and yards are surrounded
with poplar, eucalyptus, cedar, and pine plantations,
each with its windmill for raising water. It is
said that California has suffered a loss of 20,000,000
dollars (£4,000,000) this year from drought. A flock
of 500 sheep was sold recently for 600 dollars (£120),
or 4s. 9½d. a piece.

Villas became more frequent, and then the outskirts of a large town, the suburb of Oatlands, with
some manufactories, were passed, and we ran over
a long timber viaduct, with shallow water beneath
it, like the approach to Venice. One of the immense American ferryboats took us across the harbour, here three miles wide, and just as the sun
sank behind the promontory on which the capital of
the Golden Land is built, we touched the shore.

A slight sketch of the geographical position of San
Francisco may be interesting. The Pacific Ocean is
bounded at this part of California by mountain

ranges from 400 to 1,000 feet high. At one point
the continuity of this range is broken by what, if it
were not in part below the level of the sea, would
be a deep gorge with precipitous walls of rock, but
which now presents itself as the entrance to an
Inland Sea or Loch, extending to the north-east for
upwards of 30 miles, with a width varying from
three to ten miles, and to the south upwards of forty
miles, with about the same width. Most of this
great Inland Loch has a considerable depth of water.
The entrance which I have described as a partially
submerged gorge has a depth of some 250 feet. On
its northern side the cliffs and mountains behind, rise,
I suppose, nearly 2,000 feet above the water,
while on the southern shore they may be 300 feet
or 400 feet high. This entrance is about a mile
wide, and it is well named the " Golden Gate," for it
is the portal of the Land of Gold, and even if that
were not so, the fact that it forms so safe an entrance
to such a magnificent sheet of navigable inland water
would well entitle it to that name.

The City of San Francisco is situated about four
miles within this golden portal, on the southern promontory, formed by it. The water alongside the
city is deep, and the shipping lying at the wharves
are well protected from the swell of the Pacific,
which expends itself in the wide space into which it
expands. After passing the comparatively narrow
channel of the " Golden Gate," the roadstead, where
the ships anchor off the town, is deep and sheltered,
while, as in the harbours of Halifax, Boston, and

New York, unlimited wharf space is obtained by driving piles and bridging over the spaces with planks.

At San Francisco much of the lower part of the city has been won from the waters by piling and embanking. I am told that almost all the great business street of the city,—" California-street,"— was once covered by the tide.

The position of San Francisco on the western side of the inland sea I have described, and its consequent separation from the mainland of California, except by a circuit of 40 miles to the south and as many back, is embarrassing and inconvenient. The eastern shore, three miles off, would have been the proper place for the City, but the depth of water is not sufficient to accommodate shipping. They get over the difficulty, as far as possible, by the employment of steam ferryboats, which convey full train loads of railway waggons from one side of the harbour to the other. Trade coming from the south is not subject to this inconvenience.

We, in common with other produce of the East and North, had to be passed over this water space, and, as we steamed across, I little thought that we were to receive so hearty a welcome when we stepped on shore.

CHAPTER X.

SAN FRANCISCO.

IT is true that I had letters of introduction to many of the leading merchants and bankers, and we well knew that the same warm-hearted hospitality, which we had met with in other parts of America, would be extended to us here ; but I did not expect, that on stepping on shore, I should be surrounded by a crowd of ancient Cymri, some well-remembered faces, members of my old corps, and others, and that I should receive a Welshman's hearty welcome, accompanied by a bouqet of the sweetest flowers of this flowery land, a proof of kind forethought of that which would most rejoice my gentle partner's heart in this distant region.

It is difficult to say how deeply I felt the kindness of my old friends and neighbours, and still more so when a few days afterwards a deputation of 14 Glamorganshire and Swansea men, called on me in the name of the Welsh residents of San Francisco (between 400 and 500 in number) and presented me with a beautiful and costly gold-headed cane, suitably inscribed. The cane itself is made of Californian iron wood—it has a crutch handle of pure gold, at each end of which is a medallion of gold quartz ; the inner medallion opens and displays a tiny collection of the ores of California—Gold, Silver, Copper, Cinnober, (Quicksilver), Lead and Iron, each in a little triangular panel under glass.

It would be unbecoming in me to enlarge upon this personal incident, an exact paralled of which has probably never happened to any private traveller visiting a far distant land; but I may perhaps be permitted to say that the genuine and disinterested warmth of feeling which it exhibited, does honour to the ancient nation of the Cymri, and that indivi-dually I cannot be too thankful to accept it as a proof that during my three and thirty years of private work among my neighbours, and twenty-five years of public life (twenty of which as their Representative) I have succeeded in doing, what I have always earnestly endeavoured to do, " My Duty."

We passed two hours very agreeably together, talking over old days and fighting over old battles. I found that they have established a Welsh Society and that it is flourishing; I also found that, as a whole, they are doing well, and that some hold places of high trust. Two of my friends hold appoint-ments in the Mint, one is the editor of a leading journal, and some have more distant employment; one of my old workmen had journeyed 50 miles and given up two days work, to shake me by the hand. I can only say my San Francisco days will always live in my memory as the brightest of this sunshiny tour.

I was much amused by my friend, the Editor,

asking me my opinion on the burning question of
the day in Californian politics, namely, the employment of Chinese. It was rather "trying me high"
after three days residence, but I happened to be
pretty well "posted on" it, for I had been talking it
over with some of those best able to form a correct
opinion, and what they had told me appeared to be
quite sound.

No one could well treat of California, in the most
cursory manner without alluding to the Chinese.
There are 35,000 to 45,000 Chinamen and 200
Chinese women in San Francisco alone ; how many
in the whole State, I know not. They do much of
the hard work of the place, and much also of the
light or woman's work, including almost the whole of
the laundry and house work, for they are extremely
cleanly. Few Native American girls go out to
service. In the Eastern States people chiefly employ Irish girls. Imagine having to employ a raw
Irish girl to "clean" your house or "cook" your
dinner, to be thankful that you can get her at any
wages she chooses to ask, and that you are not
forced to do it yourself.

That is the condition of things as far West as
Chicago. A poor friend of mine, a resident of that
Metropolis of the West, was eloquent on the horrors
of "Irish cooking ;" but at San Francisco the Chinaman is ready to learn and to do everything ; he is
as docile as a poodle, and moves about his work as
quietly as a tame cat, always good-natured and
willing, never drunk, never away when he is wanted,

no " followers " or flirtation, no " this isn't my place," about him, ready to do anything he is told and to do it intelligently, whether it be in the house, in the field, or in the factory. His wants are few, and his vices almost none, except, indeed, opium smoking and gambling.

Without the Chinese the Great Pacific Railroad never could have been made for many years to come; the corn could not be harvested nor the grapes gathered. I saw them at work in the vineyards with the patience of women and the strength of men. Yet it is these useful labourers that the lower class of working men, the " loafers," here called " Hoodleums," wish to drive out of the country because they believe that the Chinese reduce wages, not appreciating the fact that this abundance of cheap low class labour causes the community to prosper by enabling the white man to carry out, by virtue of his natural superiority and force of character, undertakings which he could not otherwise prosecute, to enlarge those he already has in hand, to compete successfully with foreign countries, and to raise generally his own standing and position.

It is plain that California never could have risen to its present prosperity in 30 years without abundance of cheap labour. The most evil day for the white workmen of California would be that on which the Chinese left. A Chinaman gets 1 dollar per day, and finds himself; a white man, $2\frac{1}{2}$ dollars; a skilled mechanic, $3\frac{1}{2}$ dollars on the average.

An account of a visit we paid to the Chinese

quarter will be interesting. I must first explain that the Chinese occupy four "blocks" or squares of houses in the centre of the city. I believe that every block is 100 yards square, so that their quarter is only 400 by 400 yards, and in this narrow space 45,000 souls are located; yet there is but little disease and little to offend the senses. It is a garden of roses compared to many Continental towns, Berlin among the number, not to mention Cologne, Italian towns par excellence, and some French. This arises from their extremely cleanly habits. Wherever a Chinaman may be, he washes from top to toe every morning. No Europeans reside within this quarter.

The Chinese when they take to a house gut it completely. They then make two stories in place of one on each flat, then they build wooden houses in every nook and corner behind. Their rooms are mere closets, and they occupy them on the principle of "Box and Cox," "one out and t'other come in." Many work at night, and thus each limited space does double duty. Within their quarter they have shops for the sale of everything they require. Bacon and vegetables are their staples, but they are also fond of ducks and chickens.

They have regular restaurants, and we were invited by one of our friends to lunch at one in the Chinese quarter. This restaurant had a kind of cook's shop downstairs; upstairs we found ourselves in a large square room, with a wide balcony to the front, separated by a screen of open carved wood from the room behind. The screen was painted green, and

T

many parts were gilt. The walls were hung with Chinese views, and here and there mottos and notices in Chinese writing.

Luncheon was served on a long table, laid out with little dishes of sweetmeats and bouquets. The dishes were indescribable, but here is a translation of our Ménu, made by our friend's Chinese servant :—" 1, Bird's nest ; 2, Fish wing ; 3, Ham chicken ; 4, Fried dove ; 5, Fire duck ; 6, Stewed oyster ; 7, Hightoon-heyee ; 8, Mushroom ; after full of tea and cake, all kind of nut and fruit."

I did my best to taste everything, but it was a desperate effort, and for long afterwards the nauseous sodden smell stuck to me. The " bird's nest " was like a very inferior aspic jelly, with lumps of meat ; most of the other dishes were vegetables cut in slices and steeped in pork fat, bits of chicken cut round and ham glued on to them, lumps of meat and vege-tables, gelatinous croquettes with forced meat.

As far as I can remember, this is a fair description of the viands. We were also given a strong spirit called " Mong-y-lung," (not very good,) and highly scented tea. We ate with chopsticks, which are pieces of ivory thicker at one end than the other, square at the hand end ; they are used with one hand, one or more fingers being interposed to keep them apart. We really got on, as an American would say, " quite smart " with them.

I afterwards watched a dozen Chinese eating their dinner in the next room. They sat round a bowl, and, at a given signal, all plunged their chop-sticks into the bowl and fished out what they could get, which they carried to their respective plates, and ate with all kinds of little sauces and relishes, placed on little round plates ready at hand ; then all plunged again simultaneously.

Luncheon over, we adjourned to a Chinese shop, where there was nothing new, and everything double as dear as in London Chinese shops. At 8.30 p.m. we *(i.e.,* the gentlemen), accompanied by the police officer of the Chinese quarter, sallied forth to go through the dens and purlieus, and to thoroughly understand Chinese life in all its phases,

We began by visiting the Joss House, my first experience of a Heathen Temple. We climbed up a creaking staircase, walked along a stage with loose and irregular planking, and halted at a large wooden door. Our conductor gave the password and it was opened. The inside was dimly lighted, and the floor felt greasy, but all looked scrupulously clean. Opposite to us sat three grim idols, with beards, and above them burnt a lamp—a wick floating in a glass of oil—suspended by wires. This, of course, was no new sight to me. Before the altar, but at a distance of six or eight feet, was a metal screen, about four feet high and broad enough at the top to support a long tray of polished iron, filled with sand, into which Joss-sticks were thrust ; they are small slow matches, which give off a smell of incense, and keep perpetually but slowly burning down.

Inside this screen there is an elaborate representation of the history of the world, or of China, which

T 2

is the same thing in their eyes, in carved bronze —quaintly-dressed figures, some on foot, some on horseback, going through all kinds of performances, to illustrate this history. These bronze figures, which are about six inches high, are enclosed within an iron lattice work.

To the left on entering was a small cabin, in which the Chinese custodian sat, on guard. We were first introduced to two female idols on the extreme left, and were told that they were not good women; they had their sand-tray, Joss sticks and lamps burning in front of them, and were painted red and gold. All the idols are in sitting attitudes.

Passing on from left to right, we came to a male idol, who represented the God of Medicine. He held a large bolus, of the size of a cherry, in his right hand. We were next introduced to the three centre idols : the middle figure represented the God of War—a fierce fellow with a black beard. The two figures to the right and left of him are the embodiment of the Tartar and Mongolian dynasties, and are connected with the centre figure by a wide ribbon passing over their heads. We next came to the Chancellor of the Exchequer, the God of Finance and Bullion, who held an ingot of gold in his hand.

We then came to what struck me as the most remarkable idol of the whole : it represented a very good and virtuous woman, who had had a child ; it was gaudily painted and decorated with gold ; a lamp burnt above it and incense before it. Offerings of paper flowers, &c., had been made to it. I have seen hundreds of shrines so like this that I could not have told one from the other; yet I believe the Chinese religion has remained unchanged for several thousand years. I have no books to refer to, but I believe that Confucius lived more than 500 years before our Saviour, and that this religious ritual existed long before Confucius.

Beyond this female idol the next shrine was dedicated to the God of Beasts, and he had near him a small figure on horseback, brandishing an immense sword, representing the slayer of beasts. There was also a very ugly mis-shapen figure of an animal, to which they offered bacon; he generally has a large piece on his nose, which in time became so saturated that the rats ate it. The Chinese never clean or dust these idols, and they have not repaired the rat-eaten nose.

In a corner, and not in a line with the other shrines, there is a small shrine, and within it a full length standing figure of an old man, a sort of hermit, to which they pay much veneration. Every-thing in this Joss house came from China. Our guide told us that the common Chinamen know little of religion, that their festivals are rare and at irregular intervals, and that they appear not to pray much when in the Joss house. Surely, if that be so, the presence of such a large number of Chinese ought to offer great facilities for their conversion, and the sending back of native Christian mission-aries to China.

We descended the creaking stairs and entered the

sleeping quarters, the ramifications of which are of unknown extent. They appeared to sleep on raised benches of wood, covered with matting, the bed-clothes in the day-time being neatly rolled up and stowed on shelves, somewhat as in our prisons. We then went through the worst portion of the quarter, which appeared to be perfectly cleanly and orderly. I confess I felt more secure in the real China of San Francisco than I should have done in its namesake nearer home, even had I been under the able leader-ship of Superintendent Wren.

We had still to visit the opium dens. Perhaps most of my readers know as little of opium smoking as I did, and a little description may not be unin-teresting. The opium pipe is a stick of solid, heavy wood, about the size of our largest round rulers, and some three feet long; three or four inches from one end a piece of wood, somewhat like a flat low hum-ming top, say four inches in diameter and two inches high, is stuck, peg down into the pipe stick. This disc is solid except in the centre, where there is a hole into which one might insert a cedar pencil, passing down through the peg into the pipe. The smoker lies on his side on a piece of matting; at the length of his pipe a small lamp burns, the top of the flame just level with the glass which incloses it. He has his pipe in his left hand and in his right a stiff wire, with which he extracts a small quantity of opium from a little cup about an inch deep and an inch across. He then holds it over the light, when it melts and swells like a resinous gum, emitting a

slight smoke of the odour of laudanum, not altogether disagreeable. He turns the wire round, not
permitting any of the precious gum to drop off;
when well liquified he charges the hole in the pipe
with it, and holding it to the flame, draws vigorously
at the pipe, so as to cause the flame to enter the
hole and convert the gum into smoke. During this
indraft it emits a gurgling sound. Both my friend
and myself took several long pulls at it and produced the proper gurgle, but we were in no way
affected then or afterwards. Governor S. prudently
declined.

One of the men we saw was the most inveterate of
the opium smokers of San Francisco—to affect him a
whole measure was required and he had to inhale it,
i.e., swallow the smoke. He is an excellent cigar
maker, and can earn 4 dollars per day ; but like the
drunkards of our clime he smokes away all the money
he gets. As he has no wife and family to leave
penniless and starving, his guilt is probably less
aggravated than that of our Christian sot. He did
not appear to be either stupid or emaciated. Our
guide had known him for four years and observed no
deterioration in his bodily condition. He (the guide)
told us that about 75 per cent. of the Chinese smoke
opium, and that it incapacitates them, in a great
degree, from vices to which other nations are prone ;
if they drink, they do so in their own beds, buying
as much spirits as they can afford, and drinking
secretly. We did not see one drunken Chinaman
during our visit to California. It is a very remark-

able fact that only six police officers are required to keep 35,000 able-bodied Chinamen in order. At present, owing to the disturbances in the country, there are supposed to be 10,000 extra Chinese in San Francisco.

I must not omit to mention one of the most curious sights of the Chinese quarter, viz., the Theatre. We visited it in spite of having been warned in England that every conceivable disease was to be contracted at it, which is a myth. It is arranged like our theatres, except that it is all pit and gallery, with two small boxes for strangers. We found it crammed with Chinese. We could not make out the meaning of the " representation ;" I cannot use any word familiar to us without conveying a false meaning ; men and women came on to the stage and went through all kinds of by no means dumb show, for the noise was deafening from gongs, cymbals, and stringed instruments of all shapes, played on with bows, the strings of the bow being under those of the instrument. Four or more persons acted, while a kind of orchestra sat behind, the leader perched on a high stool. The actors marched in, talked and gesticulated in an excited manner for five or ten minutes, and then were succeeded by others ; while from time to time the orchestra emitted the most discordant but exciting sounds. There seemed to be a mendicant, a mandarin with two ladies and a great God, or some other *Deus ex machinâ*, dressed like the Fire King at Cremorne, but what he or they were about we none of us could make out, nor could we detect the least plot or scheme. I am told they give whole Reigns of Emperors, and that a play may last for months.

After the stricter drama came tumblers who risked their vertibræ on hard boards. They were not up to the mark of either our clowns or the Japanese at the Aquarium.

Nor must I omit a word or two on the way in which the Chinese emigration and remigration are arranged. There are several companies, I believe three, of Chinese organisation, which undertake to bring their contrymen to California and to return them alive or dead to China. The would-be emigrant agrees to pay a certain weekly sum to the company for a certain number of years, and the company agrees to find him work and protection. The bargain is faithfully kept, and, after the term is worked out, the man is free. If anyone wants a job of any magnitude to be done, he goes to the company and makes his bargain for so many hands. A Chinaman always looks to returning home after he has made money; he believes that the Spirits of the departed hover around the bones and rubbish which once held them, and thus the idea of being " out in the cold" is unpleasant to him. Few of them bring their wives, although some of those who have become rich do so. They frequently go back to China and return again to California. They are to be seen all through the State, in every small town and village, and also in Nevada and Colorado. It is probable that, except at Melbourne and Hong Kong, a

U

a bear garden among business men.   What our Capel Court may be I know not, for into that mysterious Temple of Mammon no outsider may enter without fear of assault and battery to his headgear, I am told; but at San Francisco a gallery is provided, from which the stranger can calmly survey the arena below, and an odd sight it is.   At a high bar-like table sit four clerks and a chairman, raised some 10ft. above the arena.   Around it, and raised by a few steps, are rows of armchairs.   On these, respectable-looking frock-coated gentlemen sit.   The chairman sounds an electric bell; some one shouts out the name of a Stock; up spring a certain number of the broadcloth-covered gentlemen, who rush into the arena, and commence a free fight, in the nature of what our plunger officers call "a bear fight."   They push each other about, shout at the top of their voices, set upon one man like the canine species when one has seized a bone, and, after a few minutes of chaos, some retire discomfited to their seats, while others rush excitedly to the president, and apparently record their transactions.   The bell rings again, and the same scene recurs with another Stock.   After a time one of the recording angels reads the upshot of the various encounters with extraordinary rapidity, and the wheel of fortune, or the roulette, begins to spin again.

The speculation in Mining Stocks is keen and constant.   I have a list of 201 before me; and, so far as I can learn, the same uncertainty as to the value of the best mines, the same failures and

disappointments, and the same questionable practices, prevail as with us, although trumps here mean
four honours and nine others.   We have been most
kindly received and hospitably entertained this very
day by an Irish gentleman, who is supposed to be
receiving £900,000 per annum from his share in the
great Comstock Mine, here known as the Consolidated Virginia and California Mines.   Of this also
more hereafter.

We made several interesting excursions from San
Francisco.   Our first was to the well-known Cliff
House, on the other side of the Promontory, facing
the Pacific Ocean.   Our road lay through the Park
of the City, a space won from a barren stony desert
and dunes of sea sand, now rapidly becoming clothed
with flowers and specimen shrubs.   After a drive of
a few miles, we saw the Pacific Ocean before us to
the westward, and it was indeed natural to me again
to look out to the westward, upon what our novel-
writing Premier called the " Melancholy Ocean," to
which he attributed all the ills of Ireland with
what I always accepted as the ludicrous sarcasm
of which he is a master.   However, here we were,
with the Ocean to the west of us again, but not
looking over, as we do, at the New World of far
America, but at the Ancient Empires of China,
Japan, and India, and at our own young and vigorous
Colonies of the Antipodes.

We reached the shore, and drove along the yellow
sands—just as at home—and then climbed a steep,
rocky headland on which the Cliff House Hotel is

perched, overhanging the sea. Close to it, within say four hundred yards, are three rocky islets, upon which the famous sea lions disport themselves quite at their ease, and regardless of man's proximity, for they know that the law protects them. They are a large species of seal, and we were greatly interested in watching their proceedings through our opera glasses. There might have been 100, or perhaps double that number. Some lay asleep on the rocks, some played with each other, and uttered unearthly sounds, approaching the bellowing of oxen; some swam about in the surf, now climbing on to the rocks, and then taking headers into the deep water. Like human beings, they have various orders and degrees of precedence, and jealousy prevails. The powerful old sea dogs usurp the most comfortable quarters, and woe betide the youngster who ventures to dispute their sway. Fights and romps alternate among these unlettered denizens of the deep. About 25 miles off there is a small island, upon which they congregate in thousands. We saw a few which I believe to have been the fur-bearing seal, the skin of which furnishes our ladies with their admirable winter jackets; but hereabouts they are scarce.

Another excursion was made in the Admiral's Launch up the Eastern arm of the inland sea to Mare's Island and Vallejo, where the United State's Pacific Navy Yard is situated. Fine hills surround this branch of the harbour on all sides. At its eastern end the Sacramento River enters the sea. We found that there was literally no work being

done in this or any of the United States dockyards.
It did not appear to me that there were more than a
dozen men in the shops, which were well arranged,
but not extensive.   There were a few old-fashioned
wooden ships in ordinary, and one old iron monitor
housed over.   I am told that this is the condition of
the United States' Naval Establishments everywhere.
Certainly it is so at Boston.   They are paying off
their Debt ! ! !   Congress will not vote supplies of
an adequate amount for the most moderate expenditure on the Navy and Army, and the result is that
they have no fleets, no men, and an Army reduced
to ludicrously small numbers—I believe to not more
than 25,000 men all told.   The Army pay is now
three months in arrear, Congress only having voted
nine months' supplies.   The Western Members know
nothing of the Navy, and care less for it ; and there
is a general dislike to increasing the Army.

CHAPTER XI.

WE made another interesting excursion in the same direction, landing at Vallejo, and proceeding some distance by rail to a place called Napa, from whence we drove over to the old Mexican town of Sonoma, and visited on the way the Vineyard of Buona Vista. We then returned to Napa, and ran up the valley to Calistoga. Some of the best vineyards of California are situated in these two valleys. Indeed, about Sonoma, the country is one large vineyard to the foot of the hills. The vines looked healthy, and laden with grapes, which Chinamen were busily picking. The grape most extensively grown is a black grape, called the " Mission Grape," because it was introduced orginally by the Spanish missionaries, but other and better varieties, such as my old friends the " Traminer" and " Riesling" of the Rhine, the " Muscat " the " Sweetwater," and " Tokay " all flourish. The wines are really good ; the white wines resemble " Chablis." The red wines partake more of the character of Burgundy than of Claret. They also make very good Champagne. Californian gentlemen are too chivalrous to give the wines of their own country to their friends, but let me assure them that they may do so with perfectly clear consciences, for they are excellent ; sound honest wines which need no bush—we drank nothing else while in California.

I believe the production of wine is destined to become one of the most important industries of California. To show to what an extent it has already grown, I may mention that Messrs. Groezinger, whose establishment we visited in the Napa Valley, make on an average 400,000 gallons annually. California also exports grapes on a large scale to the Eastern States ; we saw them packing a truck which carried ten tons, net, of grapes ; they put them in skeleton cases, which are screwed together and to the sides of the truck, so that the whole of the inside becomes one solid mass of grapes supported on lath frames. The truck has a false roof and sides which are filled with ice, and in this way the grapes travel without injury to New York. At starting they are worth one penny per lb. ; at what price they are retailed in New York I do not know.

The Valley of Napa is very lovely, highly cultivated and fertile, well timbered with live oak dotted about and forming picturesque groups, as in the old parks of England ; the mountains rise two or three thousand feet on each side of the valley, their sides clothed with fine timber and their rugged peaks standing sharply out against the clear blue sky.

At the end of the railway, as at present constructed, is the lovely little Watering place called

W

Calistoga, which deserves to become one of the most
famous of the American Continent.   It possesses
springs of the sulphuretted hydrogen order, hot
enough to boil an egg, and to be used as vapour
baths.   The scenery around is really magnificent—
perpendicular precipices of basalt wall it in to the
north-east, while behind rises a mountain of first-
class magnitude ; to the west the gentler hill-side
is clothed with pine woods to its summit.   I never
saw a lovelier spot ; but unfortunately it got into
bad hands and was disreputably conducted, so
that it has come to grief, and now awaits the " ex-
ploitation " of a speculator, combined with a fashionable doctor, to declare its waters capable of curing
all ills, and to condemn his victims to its noxious
potations.

We were accompanied by Mr. Towne, the able
manager of the Great Pacific System of Railways,
2,000 miles in extent ; and, among other interesting
information, he told me that a Mr. Mitchel, in the
San Joachim Valley, has 90,000 acres under wheat,
and that his ambition is to have 100,000 acres ; also,
that a Dr. Glen, on the Sacramento, had 40,000
acres last year under wheat, and wanted to contract
for 20,000 tons of freight for wheat only.   The
average produce is 25 to 30 bushels per acre, but on
the very best land it sometimes runs up to 60
bushels ; he told me that he knew an instance of
land yielding 30 bushels as a first crop, and after
irrigation giving a second crop of 61 bushels the
same year.   I made a note of this at the time,

and I give my authority, lest these figures should appear too astounding for my agricultural friends, and they should set me down as of too verdant a nature.

Our last expedition was to the district lying south of San Francisco, an alluvial flat backed up by the hills which border the Pacific. Along the foot of these hills, and among their defiles, are situated the country residences of the great men of San Francisco, and very beautiful indeed they are. One of these gentlemen, Senator Sharon, hospitably entertained us, and drove us on the following day to Governor Latham's lovely residence at Menlo Park. The house is furnished in excellent taste, the choicest specimens of European art having been unsparingly provided for its embellishment, both in pictures, sculpture, and furniture; the gardens are all that could be desired, or dreamt of in an eastern dream. Indeed, this delicious climate needs but little art to produce in profuse abundance in the open air all the shrubs and flowers we most cherish. Our only regret was that the tyrant " Time" dragged us from this most enchanting spot, where we were pressed to remain for some days—indeed, had we been able, we might have spent many a pleasant month among our hospitable friends.

Perhaps our most agreeable evening we owed to the kindness of Governor Stamford, to whom the world is indebted more than to anyone else for the inception and successful carrying out of the Great Pacific Railway undertaking, of which he is still

President. His house in San Francisco would take first rank even in London, while its furniture and a fine gallery of modern pictures is equal to anything I have ever seen in our most palatial houses.

However, the time came for us to quit San Francisco, and we headed for the Yosemite Valley, the boast of California ; I would almost say of America. It lies some 250 miles south-east of San Francisco, and is approachable for the last 90 miles by stage coach only. We slept in our car at Merced, and as the day began to dawn embarked on board a Californian stage for the first time—a boat-shaped vehicle, drawn by six horses, two abreast ; four rows of seats, face forwards, each holding three passengers ; and a light leather roof with open sides protects the inmates from the sun ; no springs except a long strap of leather of six or eight thicknesses, running horizontally under each side of the boat protected us from jolts of the most spine-breaking order. The roads are villanous, the pace good, and the consequent jolting almost unendurable ; 180 miles of this kind of travelling was no joke, but the ladies stood it gallantly,

The coachman drives with three reins in each hand, and the way he handles his team would have done credit to Probet of our youth, or Jehu of old. In some places it is by no means easy work to coach the team, for the road is wide enough for one carriage only, the turns are sharp, the gradient is steep, and a precipice is often so close on one side that the slightest mistake of man or horse would be fatal.

However, up hill and down our Jehu pushed along, often furiously and always fast.

Our road lay at first over the flat plain of the San Joachim Valley, luxuriant in Spring, but now burnt to the colour of brown paper, no blade of green visible. The sheep are dying by hundreds. We passed some large flocks in the mountains, and their track was marked by the dead and dying. We sometimes counted as many as six at once which had fallen dead by the wayside. The drought this year is greater than any in the records of the Colony. They have not had rain for six months, and the winter fall was below the average. After leaving the plain, we entered on the " Foot Hills"; first rolling, stony deserts, and then higher and clothed with scrub. After a time the Ilex and a species of stone pine began to appear, and then we began to ascend the lofty mountains of the Sierra Nevada, crossing a ridge 5,500 feet above the sea. At the village of Honitas, 23 miles from Merced, we found gold digging in active operation, the men working on their own account, and from what we heard it seemed that they were doing well. We were told that they had taken out 150,000 dollars' (equal £30,000) worth in the last six weeks, and that one old man had got 25,000 (£5,000) working by himself. On the other hand, I saw a fine, strapping Cornishman (who had been injured by an explosion of dynamite two days before), who told me that he found it better to work for day wages at four dollars per day than to run the risk of working on his own account; four dollars may be

taken as an average earning, therefore, although now
and then a man may make a " lucky hit."

We visited a gold mine by the roadside, and saw
gold dust panned out.   I went down the crazy
ladder into a small opening not more than 15 or 20
feet deep, and found a lode of quartz, with a flucan
on the back, running through the killas or slate rock.
The miners told me that it had a regular strike,
proving for a long distance, and that most of the
workings about there were on it.

From this place until some miles beyond Mariposa
we passed through slate and metamorphic formations,
showing strong signs of igneous action ; all the
" gulches," or small valleys, had been worked over
for gold, and those who can recollect the early days
of California will remember the name of Mariposa as
associated with some of the richest workings.   As a
rule these " gulches" are now worked out, and gold
mining has assumed the shape of a regular industry,
carried on by scientific mining and with large capital.
I cannot help feeling that these rich deposits of gold
in California, Australia and New Zealand were the
direct means employed by God to effect the rapid
colonization of those fair but then distant and un-
peopled lands ; and that having served their beneficent purpose, they were so designed as no longer to
affect the ordinary course of industry by attracting
too many labourers into one description of harvest,
nor to disturb the value of the precious metal, now
almost universally used as the standard of exchange
between nations and individuals.

Gold had a further and scarcely less important bearing on the rapid development of these regions. The first easily-got metallic riches of California afforded the capital by which its other latent resources have been so rapidly developed. There is many a man in San Francisco, now so rich as to be ill-described as a millionare, who began thirty years ago as a gold-digger or as a store keeper to supply the digger's wants. Now the day of the poor man and the easily-got gold is over. The country and its commerce and industries have settled down into the ordinary routine of human communities.

The "gulches" we passed were for the most part narrow, the old workings not extending over perhaps more than 20 or 30 yards in width, and it was curious to observe how the gold appeared to have settled down in the deepest part of the valley alone. Another remark of some interest I think I may venture on, viz., that the gold-bearing bottoms are, or were, either on or below the level of the clay slate or silurian formation, and that when, as on the higher lands of the Sierra Nevada, granite takes the place of slate, the gold deposits altogether cease; thus the Yosemite valley, and the bottom lands adjoining have never been worked. My guide was an old gold-digger of twelve years' experience, who had worked over the whole districts, from Dutch Flat down some hundreds of miles, and had "broke" himself prospecting, drinking and gambling. When I asked him how it was that the Yosemite bottom lands had never been worked, he said because there was nothing but granite above them, and that gold in paying quantities was never found in granite.

As to the quartz lodes being the gold bearers, I also take leave to say that I believe that both the quartz and the gold were originally contained in the slate rocks, and that they have been concentrated simultaneously in the fissures of the clay slate strata upon Mr. Fox's theory. If this be so, much of the gold found in the bottoms was probably never combined with quartz in " reefs " or " lodes," but existed in the clay slate strata, and was deposited in the bottoms during its denudation through countless ages.

The quartz lodes are extremely hard, and do not exist in sufficient quantity to account for the gold in the ancient water courses. Unfortunately, I was not able to visit the great gold mining districts of Dutch Flat, Bloomfield and Gravels, &c., because they are all now standing idle from want of water. There is a remarkable mine not far from the Yosemite, of which I saw an account in a local paper. It is called the " Standard Gold Mine" at Bodo in Mono county. On September 14th it returned 38,039 dols.; on the 25th September, 41,519 dols.; on October 5th, 73,800 dols., say £30,000 in a month, a small local affair !!!

In spite of such exceptionally brilliant mines, the total production of California proper is not now one-third what it was some years ago. In 1853 it reached 68,000,000 dols., while last year it was only 19,000,000 dols., and for ten years it has not exceeded 25,000,000 dols. ; the ten preceding years averaged upwards of 50,000,000 dols. I am thus, I think, justified in saying that gold having satisfied the beneficent end for which it was placed within man's reach with less than average toil, has now taken its place among the ordinary industries of California. The figures I have just quoted refer to California proper, and not to Nevada, which has come in to make up the deficit, having last year produced 49,300,000 dols. in gold and silver bullion owing to the immense output of the Comstock run of mines ; but there it is produced by regular mining, not by independent " Placer work," and therefore does not affect my argument. I learn from the highest authority that precisely the same condition of things has supervened in Victoria (Australia) ; the easily got gold has been worked out, and the production has fallen from £12,000,000 to £4,000,000, obtained by regular and expensive mining—but then the clip of wool has taken the place of gold.

To return to our Yosemite trip. The further and higher we advanced up the slopes of the Sierra Nevada the more densely the mountains became clothed with forest, while the trees appeared to attain a larger size, until we reached a region of veritable giants—such pines I never saw or dreamt of. I do not speak of " The Big Trees," but of the ordinary pines and firs, an enumeration of which may interest some of my readers. Almost all these pines are old friends of mine, and many can be seen in full vigour in the Singleton Pinetum. The Yellow Pines (not of

X

Canada), Pinus Ponderosa and P. Jefferyii; the Sugar Pines, P. Lambertiniana and P. Monticola; the Douglas Spruce, Abies Douglasii; the Silver Fir of California, Picea Amabilis; the Balsam Fir, Picea Grandis, and the Cedar, Libocedrus Decurrens, all grow to an extraordinary size, with the exception of the latter—hundreds of each may be seen eight feet and even more in diameter, and 200 feet and upwards in height. The Libocedrus does not grow quite so large. These Pines begin to flourish at about 3,000 feet, and I saw no diminution in their size at 6,500 feet above the sea. It was an immense treat to me to see these great trees in their fullest development, after having watched them as infants and striplings at home, and now, having seen them in their native grandeur, I shall watch them with double interest in their exile.

The sun set and left us in the midst of these splendid forests, but the moon was brilliant; our driver and his horses knew the road, and we dashed down the steep descent of 1,500 feet, round sharp curves and zig-zags, at the rate of ten or twelve miles an hour, until we found ourselves at our night's resting place, a comfortable single story frame house called " Clark's." After a really hard journey of 13 hours, early to bed and an early start for the " Big Trees " was the order of the day.

The gray dawn was just breaking as we mounted our stout little mustangs, settling ourselves for the first time on or in the old high-peaked Mexican saddles, and winding in single file along a steep mountain path through the same forest of giant firs we had traversed the night before. Soon we heard a well known sound, a pack of hounds in full cry ! ! a pack of hounds in this wild mountain region ! no, our guide tells us it is a pack of wolves hunting a deer, but no one could have told the difference of their music.

After two hours ride we reached the far-famed Mariposa Grove of " Wellingtonia Gigantea," or as the Americans incorrectly call them " Sequoia Gigantea ;" that name was given to the Red Wood Tree of California before the Wellingtonia was discovered, of which there is ample proof. Six groves of " Wellingtonia" have been discovered, but that which we visited contains the greatest number, about 600 of the largest trees. A friend has since informed me that he discovered an unknown grove of Wellingtonias, and had ridden nine miles through it, in a distant part of the Sierra Nevada, and thus it is probable that more " Groves" exist.

I wish to avoid all " tall writing," and I will therefore use no epithets in regard to these trees, but will state a few facts which may convey some idea of their size. Several have fallen—the interior of one, not the largest, was burnt out, leaving a shell with sides of some thickness ; tall as I am I rode through it, as it lay on the ground, for some 40 feet, and required to stoop very slightly. I rode alongside another which lay prostrate, and, when sitting upright on my horse, my friends said that the upper portion was at least double as high as my head—

seven of us on horseback gathered together within the hollow trunk of one that is still standing and flourishing, Indian fires in byegone times having tunnelled through its trunk, but left enough to support it. Some idea of their mighty size may be gathered from these few facts.

The largest is called the "Grizzly Giant," and is reported to be 90 to 109 feet in circumference; one side of it is burnt away, and it is, therefore, not easy to measure its exact size. I measured it as fairly as I could and made it 80 feet, but I admit it may be made 90 feet with very little humouring. Now, 90 feet in circumference means 30 feet in diameter, and 30 feet means the frontage of a first-class London house. Imagine a London house built up 325 (nearly the height of St. Paul's) very slowly tapering, and you then have before you the section which these trees would represent if cut down the centre and left standing.

A large Ocean Steamer may be 300ft. long, and 30 or 40ft. beam. Imagine it standing vertically on its stern. Imagine a round red granite column like the Duke of York's monument, but 30 feet in diameter, bare as that column for 200 feet, and then a branch 8 feet in diameter, that is larger than the largest tree you, perhaps, ever saw, shooting out horizontally, and you have a picture of the " Grizzly Giant." We gazed in wonder at these trees, and wandered about the grove trying to find cones which had not shed their seed, so that we might recreate it in miniature for our children's children in a far

distant land; not for our children's children, for
these trees are estimated to be the growth of from
1,500 to 4,000 years. If that be so, more than a
thousand generations must pass away before their
like can be seen in England.

It interested me much to take note of the conditions under which they grow. I had heard that
they grew in a valley; that is not so; they grow
on a ridge 6,600 feet above the sea, and 2,600 feet
above the valley in which we slept. They do not
crown the ridge, but are slightly on the south side
of it. The hills at a distance rise higher in almost
all directions it is true, and they may thus be
sheltered to some extent. Most of the trees grow
on an outlying mass of silurian rock, but some few
are on granite. The soil is damp, in spite of the
want of rain for six months; in fact, a fine spring of
water bursts out in the thickest portion of the
grove; they evidently do not flourish where the soil
is very dry. Most of the trees have passed their prime
and are going off, and it is remarkable how small
their foliage is as compared to their bulk. I cannot
say that I saw more than one flourishing young tree.

Taking leave of this wonderful grove, we retraced
our steps and embarked in our six-horsed boat for
the Yosemite Valley, which is in fact the North Fork
of the Merced River, we having passed our night at
"Clark's," on the South Fork. Our road lay over the
dividing spur, and reached an elevation of 5,500
feet, the bottom of the Yosemite Valley being 4,050
above the sea.

Having seen the great valleys of Switzerland, the Tyrol, Italy, Styria and Norway, I wondered whether so *blasé* a traveller, as I fear I am, could find any novelty in the Yosemite ? My verdict is that it is in many respects novel and much to be admired : the Romsdahl in Norway, where the Troll Tinder and Romsdahl Horn rise in sheer precipices 3,500 feet out of the valley, and where, for 20 or 30 miles, the sides are too precipitous to allow of egress, approaches most closely to the Yosemite, but the latter has peculiar and very marked features of its own. It is a deep rent in a compact white granite formation. On all sides the precipices are sheer and brilliantly white, while the valley, the tops, and here and there the lateral ravines, are clothed with the splendid pines and firs which I first described.

The granite, an igneous formation, rent asunder probably by the contraction of the earth's surface in cooling, has formed domes and peaks, rising like spires from 3,000 to 5,000 feet from the valley below. "El Capitan" juts out a sheer and massive granite cliff 3,300 feet high ; opposite to him, and retiring from his bold advance, are the "Three Graces," 3,400 feet high ; sheltering beneath them are the "Cathedral Spires," 2,600 feet, rising in needle points ; while on the opposite side the "Three Brothers," 3,900 feet, out-top the stalwart Captain and gaze across at "The Three Graces," never however to be re-united until perhaps the crack of this world's doom shall sound and rend the universe asunder, causing the precipices to topple to their downfall. In the centre of the valley, on its southern side, stands the lone "Sentinel," 3,100 feet, an isolated rock towering above the comfortable shanty where we passed the night. 1,000 feet above and behind him rises the "Sentinel Dome."

Ascending the valley, we have on the left the North Dome, 3,725 feet, and on the right the South Dome, 5,000 feet, which can only be ascended by ropes and ladders. The highest mountain of all closes in the valley to the East, and is well named "Cloud's Rest;" it is 6,150 feet above the valley, and 10,190 feet above the sea. Beneath the two domes is Mirror Lake, a beautiful little sheet of water, so sheltered, calm and clear, that it reflects the precipices above it with such perfect sharpness and truth that one hardly knows whether one is gazing at the mountain itself or its reflection. The well known photographs of "Mirror Lake" give the effect truthfully, and may be viewed either side up with almost equal effect.

We had but one day to stay in this wondrously beautiful valley, and it was a question whether we should climb the lofty "Sentinel Dome" or wander through the valley and thoroughly and quietly enjoy its beauties. Our friends chose the former, and describe the views of the distant Sierra and the Foot-hills, almost down to the Pacific, as magnificent, not omitting the domes and peaks of the valley itself below them. We chose the latter, and were equally content with our ride through the lovely park-like scene, and our quiet study of the beauties of the valley itself, the towering precipices above us, and the tall trees around us.

I cannot, alas, describe the waterfalls, for there was "a strike on," and they had ceased to work!! The "Bridal Veil," 940 feet, was alone running a few gallons, not enough to shelter the Bride's blushes. The picturesque part of the Yosemite Valley is but eight miles long, after which, in each direction, it becomes a gorge, or canyon as it is here called.

The Yosemite was our most distant point, and we here began our "back trail," which we have already followed for some 1,100 miles, during which journey most of what I have recorded, beginning with San Francisco, has been written.

CHAPTER XII.

NEVADA SILVER MINES.

I HAVE still to describe our visit to the great Nevada Silver Mines on the "Comstock" lode. Our kind friends of the Central Pacific Railway gave us a "special" to Truckee (177 miles), which saved us a day, and enabled us to see the portion of the Sierra Nevada by daylight which we had before passed in the night. We were also permitted to stop our train at the most interesting points.

I can only describe this portion of the route, *i.e.*, for some 20 or 30 miles on either side of the summit of the Sierra Nevada, as very fine mountain scenery, but without the lofty rugged peaks of Switzerland or the bold outlines of Norway. The pine forests have been largely cleared close to the line, but some giants of the same species as those we passed on our way to the Yosemite, still remain. Donner Lake, just below the summit to the east, is a beautiful sheet of water, embosomed in trees, but of no great extent. It was the scene of a sad tragedy in early emigrant days : a large party having been overtaken by snow and starved to death. The "summit" itself of the Sierra Nevada does not afford a striking view on either side ; it is compact white granite, just like the backbone of old Cornwall.

Y

At Truckee we left the Pacific line, and, sending our car round to Carson City, drove up a fine woodland valley by a clear stream to Lake Tahoe, the highest lake in the world on which a steamer plies. It is 36 miles long, 9 or 10 broad, and about 7,500 feet above the level of the sea; its depth is said to be 1,700 feet, and I was told by several people that the best swimmer cannot remain long above the water; a man who cannot swim never rises if he falls into it. The Indians will not venture on it; its name means "The Evil One;" it is the only lake I have seen in America which reminded me of Switzerland. The dividing ridge of the Sierra Nevada forms its western shore, rising many thousand feet above it, and terminating in fine irregular outlines.

We sped across its deep blue waters in a high-pressure steam-launch at the rate of some 15 miles an hour, and on landing found to our surprise a locomotive waiting to push us up a zig-zag narrow-guage line to the top of the ridge which divided us from Carson Valley. This line forms part of a great undertaking for the supply of the Silver Mines of Virginia city with timber, its object being to convey the timber cut upon the borders of the Lake to the top of the ridge, from whence it is floated down in what are called "Flumes," to the Carson and Virginia City Railroad. These "Flumes" are angular launders of wood, with enough water flowing through them to float the timber, which shoots down them at from 10 to 12 miles an hour, and is landed at

Carson, 13 miles away, without the hand of man ever touching it.

The zig-zags were arranged so that the engine reversed itself at each turn, and first pushed and then pulled us. The line was most expensive to construct, having cost £7,000 per mile ; and, with all due deference, I fancy a fixed engine and incline would have answered every purpose at a quarter of the first and working cost. The whole face of the country was denuded of trees, and looked most forlorn. Soon the beautiful shores of Lake Tahoe will be equally spoiled, for the maw of the mines is insatiable.

At the top we found another six-horse coach, steered by the most famous whip of the West ; and away we went down the steepest hill and worst road I ever travelled over, until we reached the Carson Valley, 1,500ft. below. A night in our car, and then an early start for Virginia City, a city literally built upon the greatest silver and gold mines in the world. After 20 miles of rapid ascent and sharp curves, we were in the midst of this " mine of wealth." On the way we had passed several quartz mills for stamping and amalgamating the Comstock ores. We also passed not a few mining claims, which appeared to consist of a white board with a name painted on it, and nothing more. Among others, I saw my own name posted up, indicating the nation and country from which the claimant came. Cornishmen are the best miners, and are more numerous than any other race in the mining world of the West. The poverty of Cornwall has created the wealth of Western America.

We ran through the extensive mining town of " Gold Hill," and pulled up almost at the office door of the Consolidated Virginia and California Mines, beyond all question the two richest mines in the world. The produce of the first in 1876 was 16,657,649 dollars, = £3,331,529, and of the latter 13,386,956 dollars, = £2,677,391, or a total of upwards of six millions sterling. These two mines are in fact one, and belonged to a great extent to the same owners, being worked from the same shaft, and the produce kept separate as a matter of account. Shares are sold separately in each, but they may be viewed as a whole when speaking of them as a mine. The length of both sets together is only 1,500ft., or 250 fathoms.

The whole country for miles round is of a highly igneous geological character. In the valley between Truckee and Tahoe Lake I saw actual volcanic tufa, and as we approached Virginia City the rocks were syenitic and porphyritic; a precipitous hill, Mount Davidson, of the same formation (syenite), about 1,500ft. high, rises immediately above the mines.

Mr. Mackay, an Irish gentleman, who owns a very large interest in these so-called Great Bonanza Mines, which are supposed at this time to be yielding him a clear profit of £900,000 per annum, probably the largest income in the world, very kindly donned his miner's dress, and took us underground, leading the way, and showing a perfect knowledge of every part

we visited. They call the ore ground here a " ledge,"
and I shall use that word, for I know no mining term
in common use which properly describes it.
We descended in a cage like that of a coal mine,
sunk vertically to the east of the " ledge," which
underlies in that direction at 45 degs. The pit will
intersect it at, I think, 2,000ft. They have cross cut
to it at various levels, their last being 1,750ft. We
went to the 1,650ft. as the lower level has only
recently cut the " ledge," which has a north and
south strike. We first went to the end of a half-
course drift, which was being driven in barren ground
to take air to the face, and was then, I should say,
60 yards " before the air" without a brattice. At
the end of this drift the temperature appeared to me
to be as hot as the last chamber but one of a Turkish
bath. Unfortunately, I did not take a thermometer
down with me. Many places in these mines are so
hot that men can only work for a quarter of an hour
at a time, and then they require quantities of iced
water and iced air. This mine alone uses ten tons
of ice per day. Pouring iced water over the wrist
produces an extraordinary tingling sensation. The
can of iced water appears to steam from the con-
densation of the watery vapour around it. The
great heat is no doubt in part due to the natural and
constant increase of temperature as you descend.
As far as I remember, the general law of the in-
crement of heat we established by our investigations
in the coal commission was, " a normal temperature
of 50 degs. at 50 feet., and then one degree (Fahren-

heit) for every 50ft. in depth. Therefore at 1,650ft., we should have 50 degs. plus 32 degs.=82 degs.—but I am sure the heat in the Bonanza mine must have been over 100 degs. Whether the excess is due to the igneous nature of the formation, or to the chemical action of the vein stuff, I know not.

Mr. Mackay told me that the "ledge" is about 1000ft. broad, but that the ore bearing or paying portion varies in their mine from 70ft. to 360ft., being extremely irregular. It is sometimes divided by "Horses," *i.e.*, wedges of barren ground, and he showed me one 70ft, wide in the midst of the ore ground. They take all the ore ground away in its full width, be it wide or narrow, and cross cut to prove the barren parts of the "ledge." As they take it away so they fill in the space quite full of timber, about a foot square, laid horizontally ; the mainways are kept open by the heaviest timbers close together, accurately morticed, and yet they crush.

The "ledge" of ore ground is composed of nodules, or small irregularly-shaped pieces of greenish-drab rock, surrounded by "sugary" quartz. The quartz is not compact and hungry looking, but very friable. Sometimes the quartz and sometimes the drab stones predominate ; the quartz does not carry the ore to any extent ; it is almost wholly contained in the drab stone, which Mr. Mackay said was "porphyry." After carefully examining it under a magnifying glass, I think that it is of that nature, that is to say, something between Cornish elvan and tufa.

I can detect minute spots of dark ore, which I take to be sulphide of silver. I also see spots of iron and copper pyrites, some bright spots may be native silver, but I doubt it. I think I can detect in the specimens I have one minute piece of gold; but as the ore contains only $2\frac{1}{2}$ ounces of gold per ton, it may well be in combination with the silver, copper, and iron sulphides, for it is perfectly well established that gold will go into such combinations with other metals. The average contents in silver are about 40 or 50 ounces per ton. The ore averages in value about 100 dollars (£20) per ton, of which about 45 per cent. is gold, and 55 per cent. silver.

Mr. Mackay informed me that the lying wall of the ledge is syenite, while the hanging wall is a kind of clay, marked truchite, greenstone, and porphylite on Mr. Sutro's section. The character of this occurrence of ore is evidently very exceptional, and I cannot pretend to offer an opinion on its origin, except that as the ore ground is confined to one side of the ledge, it would seem as if the strata it is in contact with on that side must have had something to do with the presence of ore in that part of the ledge. The two great mines nicknamed "The Bonanza," from that word signifying in Mexican a great bunch or deposit of ore (or possibly "goods"), are by no means the only ones on this ledge. Eight adjoining mines last year produced 7,569,798 dollars (£1,513,959) of gold and silver bullion. Some of these mines have been extraordinarily productive in past times, but have now "cut poor" for this district, although two, viz., the "Belcher" and "Ophir," produced more than one-half the above sum last year. It is stated on a map, obligingly given me by Mr. Sutro, that up to 1st April, 1870, the Comstock lode had yielded 120,250,000 dollars (£24,500,000) of gold and silver bullion. Its produce since that time has been much greater, but I am not in possession of the figures.

It will be seen that the ore itself is not rich, being worth on an average £20 per ton, while silver ores sometimes run as high as £2,000 or £3,000 per ton. It is the quantity produced which constitutes the richness of these mines. The Consolidated Virginia and California alone are now raising no less than 1,400 tons per day, or £28,000 gross, from which must be deducted the loss of metal (equal to about one-tenth) and the cost of getting the ore and "returning" the bullion. This production is much in excess of that of any previous period.

As to the future of this run of mines, it would be presumptuous on my part to speak after a day's visit. Give me the run of the mines and maps for a month, and I might hazard an opinion; it is plainly an uncertain "bunchy" ore occurrence. I observe on Mr. Sutro's section of 1870 that the blanks at that time outnumbered the prizes, obtained by sinking on 17,000 feet of the run of the Comstock lode, as four or five to one. There appears to be no regularity in the occurrence of the ore, but when it does occur it is in great masses. I am sorry that I can give no more definite prophesy, because the future of this great bullion production is of world-wide interest, being supposed to be one of the disturbing elements in the value of silver. Seeing, however, that nearly one-half the value of the produce of these mines is gold, I incline to think that their disturbing influence must have been over-rated.

In speaking of the future of these mines I ought not to overlook the great work of Mr. Sutro, who obtained an Act of Congress enabling him to drive a deep "Adit," or Tunnel, nearly four miles long, to unwater the mines, at a depth of 2,244 feet. It is evident that this "Adit" must relieve the mines of a great charge for pumping water, and enable many a poor mine to struggle on and perhaps cut rich again. Moreover, I think it probable that it will become a great in-take airway, and give the mines an abundant supply of fresh air in their bottom levels.

A few words as to the extraction of the gold and silver: this is effected by the old amalgamation process, which depends upon the affinity of gold and silver for quicksilver. The ore is stamped wet to a fine slime, then run into circular iron vats about four feet high, and five feet diameter, closed over with sheet iron. The stuff is kept in a constant state of agitation by fans revolving in the vats. Quicksilver is added, as also sulphate of copper and salt. The liquid is heated by steam. The well-known chemical reaction takes place, setting free the gold and silver from their primary combinations, and enabling them to combine with the quicksilver, which is then run off, and the uncombined portions of quicksilver

z

allowed to filter through close linen bags, the amalgam of gold, silver, and quicksilver remaining behind, from which the quicksilver is expelled by heat, in retorts, in the usual way, leaving the gold and silver in such a state as to require only to be melted into ingots. The merits of this process are the saving of labour and fuel, both very costly in this country, and the rapidity of extraction of the precious metals. The demerits are, great loss of quicksilver, amounting at this mine to £15,000 per month, and loss of produce in slimes and tailings, equal to eight dollars or 10 dollars, say 30s. to 40s. per ton of stuff. I am by no means prepared to say that I could not suggest two or three better modes of treatment, but it would be too big an affair for any one to undertake, especially in view of the uncertainty of these mines, and the cheapness and facility of the present process as to labour, fuel, and returns.

Leaving Virginia City we rejoined the main line of the Union Pacific at Reno, and were soon " hitched " on to a regular Express and well on our homeward way ; three days and nights brought us to Cheyenne on the Union Pacific Railway, from whence we diverged from our old route in a due southerly direction to Denver, 106 miles distant. Up to Cheyenne I have already described our route over vast and dreary sage brush plains, relieved only by the passage of the Palissade, Weber, and Echo Canyons, and the fine mountains about Salt Lake, now powdered with their first snows.

From Cheyenne to Denver our route lay parallel

with the great chain of the Rocky Mountains, the highest peak of which here rises 9,000 feet above the plain and 14,000 feet above the sea. This range is really Alpine in its height and outline. Several peaks, in fact, exceed 14,000 feet, the highest being Pike's Peak 14,336 feet ; the range is intersected by deep canyons or ravines, and at four or five places, forms secluded, so-called " Parks," which I am told are very beautiful, being flat, grassy, park-like spaces, as large as Glamorganshire, embosomed in lofty mountains, and well timbered up to 10,000 feet. Three of these peculiar parks, called North, Middle, and South Parks, have been set apart for the use of the public for ever—one, Este's Park, about 500,000 acres in extent, I am told, and containing within it one of the loftiest mountains of the range, (Long's Peak) 14,050 high, has been purchased by the Earl of Dunraven, whose admirable work, " The Great Divide," is so well known and appreciated. North Park is about 70 miles long and 23 wide.

Time would not permit us to visit any of these lovely spots. We had but one day, and we spent it in plunging deep into the Rocky Mountain range. Leaving Denver early we proceeded by broad guage (4 ft. 8½ in.) to Golden, and thence by narrow guage (3 ft.) up the Clear Creek Canyon to George-town, the central town of this Silver Mining District, and the seat of several reduction works, situated 8,675 feet above the sea by my aneroid. The little 3 ft. guage line has been carried up this chasm, so narrow at places that it would seem almost impassable for

z 2

a goat, with indomitable energy and at slight cost—
only £1,000 per mile. Some of the grades are 1 in
26, and some of the curves 36 degrees; but it works
well and pays well. The engine, with three small
coupled wheels, can take up 50 tons net.

Georgetown is 54 miles from Denver, and nine
miles only from the "Divide" of the Rocky Mountains. They intend ultimately to push their little
line through to the Salt Lake Valley, about 250
miles further. Hereafter, this route may become a
favourite one to the Pacific, for it is by far the shortest and incomparably grander than the existing line.
The Canyon at its lower end is a mere reft in a solid
"Gneiss" formation (the first of that formation which
I have seen on this Continent); the rocks appear to
impend over the narrow gorge, rising frequently in
precipices 1,500 feet above the railway—a wilder
place I never saw.

Central City and Black Hawk, the site of extensive reduction works, lie up another branch of the
Canyon. Time did not permit us to visit them.
Gold washing is prosecuted by poor men as a standing industry all along the valley in the gravel beds;
if they get four dollars per day they do well.

The Silver Mines are regular lodes, apparently
almost wholly in "Gneiss," which in its lithological
character reminded me strongly of the country around
Freiberg, in Saxony, with which, indeed, it seemed
to be identical. The ore I saw was a mixture of pure
silver ore with some galena, copper, and zinc blende,
much as in the Saxon Erzgebirge.

The whole value of metals produced in Colorado was estimated last year at 6,057,000 dollars—£1,300,000. The metalliferous mines extend all along the range of the Rocky Mountains, but the most productive district is that which we visited. On our return darkness set in before we regained Denver.

On the morrow, at an early hour, we started for our final journey eastward by the Kansas Pacific Railway, over the endless rolling prairies of Colorado and Kansas ; no more sage-brush and salt, but short nutritious prairie grass, upon which numbers of cattle feed, and here and there herds of antelopes ; we vainly bombarded them from the rear platform of our car, having an understanding with our conductor that if we killed one we might stop the train to pick it up ; but it was no joke shooting antelope at 600 or 900 yards from a jolting train going 30 miles an hour. We saw many balls strike close to them and turn them, but none took effect. We also passed two wolves within shot, but unluckily were not ready for them.

For hundreds of miles we traversed prairies without a house in sight except at the Stations of the Railway ; it is a wild country, and has a somewhat evil repute. It is said that the thirteen desperadoes who stopped and robbed a train on the Union Pacific just before we crossed to California came from this district, and last night our conductor told us to be ready, as there had been a "difficulty" with the Indians two nights before, about twelve miles from where we then were, and that they had killed two "ranche men" (a "ranche" is a farm, or "run"); they have never been known to attack a train since the early days of railways out here, and there was no real danger. However, both as we passed "out West," and on our return journey, we have had our guns and rifles ready, and should have given them a pretty warm reception.

Now we are within a few miles of Kansas City, and have been for some time running through a well-farmed rich country, the Indian corn standing thick and high, higher than a man's head on horseback. The winter wheat bright green, and the fields divided by hedges; the rivers full, for it has rained heavily, though now the sun is hot and the sky Italian; the autumn tints are on the trees and are very lovely, ripened as the foliage has been by a southern sun. Cottages and homesteads around us in all directions, —no more antelopes, wolves, Indians, or "road agents" (the American for highway robbers). We are to "mail" our letters at Kansas City, the last we shall post before we become ourselves the bearers of our own despatches.

CHAPTER XIII.

ST. LOUIS.

KANSAS CITY was reached just at sunset. We had light enough to see the fine bridge over the turbid Missouri, but neither time nor light to see the City, which appeared to be enveloped in smoke and dust, for we had again reached the great coal districts of America. Indeed, it appears from the geological map that for a long distance west of Kansas we had been passing over the coal measure formation, although I saw no evidence of it—no sidings full of coal trucks or surface indications of coal workings—nothing but rich alluvial land under cultivation, purely agricultural apparently.

The usual good night's rest on board our yacht car after our supper and our rubber, and then at early dawn we found ourselves approaching St. Louis. The country was well timbered with hard wood ; the leaves falling and the autumn tints disappearing rapidly ; fields in excellent cultivation divided by fences ; meadows in which cattle were grazing, and winter wheat of emerald green, made up the landscape, an immense relief, after the brown plains and hills of California, the dreary sage-brush desert, extending for a thousand miles more or less over which we had passed, and the scarcely more attractive rolling prairie covered with brown grass and devoid of all features of interest.

We soon arrived at St. Louis, formerly the undisputed capital of the Far West. Now its title to that distinction is sharply disputed by its great rival, Chicago.

Each of these two cities possesses special advantages. The one is the chief port of the great lakes of Northern America ; the other, situated as it is at the junction of the two main arteries of inland navigation, the Missouri and Mississippi rivers, commands the trade of the country which they intersect. Both are " located " on the borders of the Far West, and are connected with it by lines of railway bringing in to them the abundance of its agricultural produce in grain, cattle, hogs, and sheep.

The merchants and brokers of both cities gather together the units and send them forth in their organised millions. Samples of grain of all kinds are brought to the halls of their Chambers of Commerce. The hall of St. Louis is said to be the largest Corn Exchange in the world ; it is 96 feet wide, 220 feet long, and 60 high. Here grain of all kinds has its proper grade of quality assigned to it, and here it passes from the hands of the farmer to those of the exporter or miller. Hogs are gathered together in the yards, appraised at their value, and slaughtered or sent forward as I described when at Chicago. Cattle and sheep are dealt with in these great western marts in like manner.

In the year 1876 St. Louis received and dealt with

64,758,528 bushels of grain of all sorts (Chicago 87 millions). In hogs St. Louis is far behind, having received 877,160 and packed only 329,895, against two millions and a quarter at Chicago. I see the average number of hogs packed in the West is upwards of five millions per annum, and the average price last year (for 100lbs. gross) was 7.06.56 dollars, say 28s. 3¼d. or about 3½d. per pound. St. Louis received 349,043 cattle and 157,831 sheep last year, or about one-third as many cattle as Chicago and half as many sheep.

These deficiencies are compensated by its transactions in other products; thus St. Louis is the chief centre of the American lead trade, no less than 24,175 tons having passed through its markets last year; about one-half of this lead came from the west, and the other half was of local production. Cotton also figures as a large item, 244,598 bales having been received during 1876.

The growth of St. Louis has been rapid, though not so much so as Chicago. In 1799 its population was 925; 1840, 16,469; 1850, 74,439; 1870, 310,864; and it is now estimated at 495,000, while Chicago is estimated at 460,000. It was originally a French settlement, and retains some of its ancient national characteristics, especially the predominance of the Roman Catholic religion among many of its leading families. The French language is also still spoken; an old woman begged of me in French in the street.

This city is laid out in the ordinary American

way, that is, wide streets at right angles to each
other, but there is nothing especially noteworthy
that I was able to observe, except the magnificent
bridge over the Mississippi. That indeed is a grand
engineering achievement ; it consists of three spans,
two of 500 feet and one of 250 feet, and carries a
double line of railway with a 50 feet roadway over
it.

The Mississippi is an ill-conditioned mud-begrimed
turbulent stream, the most disappointing first-class
river I ever saw ; its bed is a mass of sand which at
times it scours away down to the rock. It was,
therefore, necessary to carry the stone piers deep
enough to place their foundations firmly on the rock
itself. This was effected by first building a wrought
iron caisson of the size and shape of the foundation
of each pier, viz., hexagonal and 28ft. across. This
caisson was open only at the bottom, but was furnished with a manhole at the top through which the
workmen descended into it ; compressed air was
pumped in through pipes. Walling of massive stone-
work was built upon the caisson, tier by tier, until
the caisson was sunk deep enough to reach the sand.
Then men descended into it through shafts in the
masonry, and worked the sand out by proper
mechanical arrangements, until at last the caisson
reached the solid rock ; it was then filled with con-
crete, and became as solid as the rock itself. The
shafts were likewise filled in, and the massive piers
stood and still stand defying the rush of this turbulent river. To reach the rock, and allow 50ft. clear

above the highest water level, one of these piers had
to be built 191ft. high from the bed rock, and another
165. Their weight is said to be from 28,000 to
33,000 tons.

The bridge itself depends on eight parallel arched
girders of wrought iron ; four support each railway
line, two being placed vertically, *i. e.*, one over the
other in pairs. Each pair is connected by diagonal
braces, and kept in a vertical position by very
strong distance pieces of wrought iron, stayed by cross
ties. The railways and roadways are supported by
vertical lattice girders of angle iron, rising from the
diagonal braces of the arched girders, which have all
the strain to bear. It is a very splendid piece of
work, but I fancy the present American system of
building bridges of great span is cheaper and me-
chanically better. It depends on the use of flat bars
on edge below the roadway to take the rending
strain, and light tubes above to take the crushing
strain, braced together by diagonals and uprights. I
think they beat even Brunel's Saltash and Windsor
"bow and string" bridges for lightness and economy,
which I had previously looked upon as the finest
engineering in the world. Of course such brute force
affairs as the Menai and Grand Trunk of Canada
Bridge at Montreal can only be named with bated
breath as a reproach to English engineering.

The St. Louis Bridge was built out from the piers
by *balance*, without scaffolding, that is to say, the
pier was first raised to its height, and the iron
structure was built out simultaneously on each side,

connecting rods being passed over the pier, so that every ton added on one side a corresponding ton was added on the other " to keep the balance true." It cost, I believe, about £1,000,000. The German gentleman in charge of the bridge kindly took me over it, and explained the details.

I must confess I am much disappointed with the Mississippi. I had visions of the Nile, the St. Lawrence, and the Rhine, and expected to be equally impressed. Instead of those glorious masses of rushing water, I saw a volume of liquid mud, not even of a picturesque red tinge like the Severn, but much like the Thames between London and Battersea in its times of deepest defilement. I was even disappointed in the size of the river. It is but 500 yards wide, and about 30ft. deep. I fancy that the Rhine at Cologne is wider, as deep, and quite as rapid while we all remember the comparative clearness of its waters. No doubt the Mississippi at St. Louis is a long way from its mouth, but it never can, I think, become a satisfactory river to those who cannot admire muddy water.

There is an air of business-like activity, without ostentatious display, about St. Louis, which contrasts favourably with Chicago. There is no architectural extravagance in the offices and warehouses, the outcome of fires, mortgages, and commercial excitement. All the buildings are plain and solid, as befits the object for which they are designed. The outskirts of the city are filled with substantial villas standing in their own gardens, and further afield are well

arranged parks and pleasure grounds. The Churches
are numerous and handsome; as I before said, owing
to its French origin, and to the number of Irish who
have settled there, the Roman Catholic element
seems to predominate.

Time unfortunately did not permit of my visiting
the lead and iron mines around St. Louis; in fact,
three times three months would not suffice to take
stock of the details of this great Continent; my tour
is like the first rough sketch of the artist, the details
may or may not ever be filled in.

Eastward and ever eastward is now the burthen
upon us, and so our next short halt was at Cincinnati,
after traversing the rich farming States of Illinois and
Indiana. The former is destined hereafter to be as
famous for its mineral as for its agricultural resources,
representing as it does one of the largest of the
American coal-fields. The lower portion of Indiana
also includes the Southern end of the same field.

The City of Cincinnati impressed us most favourably; indeed, it is called the "Queen City"; its
situation is certainly fine, stretching for several miles
along the North bank of the Ohio, which here bends
to the South, so that the City fills up the inner arc
of the half circle, thus fronting the river on two of
its sides. The ground rises rapidly from the river,
then flattens and rises again, causing the City to be
built alternately on terraces facing the river, and
then to cling as it were to the hill side, which rises
higher and higher until it attains an elevation of
several hundred feet.

At least one-third of the inhabitants of Cincinnati are either German or of German extraction; they live in a separate quarter on the other side of the Miami canal, which they have christened the Rhine, and the quarter they inhabit is thus " Over the Rhine." Our road to the pretty park and suburb of Clifton lay through this quarter, and one might have imagined one-self in Germany, both names and sign-boards being almost exclusively in German characters, while every third house was a " Bier Keller," or " Halle," or " Tanz Boden."

Immense breweries flourish in this part of the City, and I was told that last year 500,000 barrels of beer were brewed in Cincinnati. I can vouch for the excellence of the produce, for I have never tasted better in Munich itself. On this side of the City the hill terminates in a cliff, and on the top of it is perched one of the characteristic German Lust Häuser, where the good Deutschers assemble in summer, and drink huge glasses of frothing amber liquid (wonderfully unintoxicating, probably because made of pure malt and hops alone), to the strains of really good music, or twirl their buxom Frauen round in the old " trois temps" or " schottish" to the same strains.

Cincinnati over the Rhine took me back to happy days gone by, for I love the old Deutsche Sitten in spite of their Rauch, and old Deutschland itself in spite of its Rinnen; and verily, in Cincinnati, there are the Rinnen, dirty filthy gutters, running down the streets as odorous as in the Fatherland.

The German element appears to have imparted
much solidity to Cincinnati. No nonsensical outward show is to be seen there ; the warehouses and
offices are substantial, without display, and the
advanced position which Cincinnati takes in all that
appertains to education and the arts, is probably in
a great degree traceable to the same influence. I
have before me the Forty-Seventh Annual Report of
the Education Board of Cincinnati, and anything
more " thorough" I cannot conceive. The City
seems to be divided into 26 districts for primary
educational purposes, each provided with good and
substantial schools. Then follow four " intermediate"
schools ; then three high schools, then five schools
for " coloured" pupils, then a " deaf mute school" ;
and, lastly, a " normal school" ; also 17 night schools :
all are free, being supported by local taxation. The
examination papers in the higher " grades" of the
" high schools" are given in the Report, in Latin,
Greek, German, French, Surveying, Chemistry,
Astrology, Natural History, Mental Philosophy, Constitution, Book-keeping, Trigonometry, &c., &c. I
have been looking over the papers, and am only
thankful that my examination in them is not im-
pending. (If the Atlantic and the good ship
" Russia" behave well, I shall try to touch again on
American education before the all-absorbing duties
of home-life shunt my pen into other lines.)

Then the Public Library of Cincinnati is an object
of just pride to the good citizens. It possesses
84,602 volumes, and £4,000, raised by an infinitely

small tax on realised property, is expended annually in the purchase of new books. So much is this Library appreciated, that last year 662,407 books and periodicals were lent to the inhabitants. Besides this Public Library, there is a large Commercial Library, dependent on an annual subscription of 5 dols.—£1. There are also Schools of Art, and an immense building to be devoted to music is now in course of construction. I believe that nearly as flattering a tale might be told of many another American city.

As a seat of manufacturing industry Cincinnati ranks high. It is stated by some to rank third in commercial importance in the United States, but for that I do not vouch. Certainly its manufactures embrace a wide field. It is famous for its Breweries, Whisky Distilleries, Furniture Factories, Steamboats, Steam Engines, Church Bells, Organs, Pianos, Carriages, Trunks, Chemicals, Starch, Glue, Soap, Candles, Cooperage, Wine, Castings, Cutlery, and an endless list of other articles. It is said that from no Railway Depôt in the United States is so great a variety of articles exported.

The annual report of the Board of Trade of Cincinnati states that in 1875 it had 4,469 manufacturing establishments, with a cash capital of 63,149,085 dols. invested. The value of real estate occupied was 52,151,680 dols. There were 60,999 hands employed, and the value of the products amounted to 144,207,871 dols. The exports of 1874 were 221,536,852 dols., and the imports 331,177,055

dols. It is also a great centre for the import and
export of pig iron to the States of Ohio, Indiana,
Illinois, and Michigan—five hundred firms being
engaged in manfacturing or dealing in iron alone.
Its transactions in pig iron amount to 25,000,000
dols. annually, say £5,000,000.

The manufacturing and commercial prosperity of
Cincinnati is based on her situation on the banks of
the Ohio, which passing through one of the greatest
coal and iron districts of the United States, supplies
her abundantly and at the cheapest possible rate,
while it opens to her the riparian coasts of the Ohio,
Mississippi, and Missouri, said to be thirty thousand
miles in length, measuring, I presume, both banks of
those rivers.

The first settlement of this prosperous city was in
1788, but the early settlers had constant and bloody
encounters with the Indians, and many years elapsed
before their position became assured and peaceful.
In 1800 the population was but 750; it is now
estimated at about 300,000. The city itself is
on the right, or West Virginian bank of the Ohio,
but it is connected by a splendid suspension bridge
with the Kentucky shore, on which, immediately
opposite, is the town of Carrington. This bridge is
2,252 feet in length, 36 feet wide, and 103 feet above
the water line at low water. The central span is
1057 feet; the piers are 200 feet high; the cost was
£360,000—it is quite one of the finest suspension
bridges I ever saw.

To illustrate the advance in bridge building as to

cost, in comparison with the above and with the Mississippi bridge at St. Louis, I will give the figures of the Southern Railway Bridge now being constructed at Cincinnati over the Ohio.   It is a trestle girder bridge, and, with its approaches, will be a mile long ; it has one span of 519 feet, two of 300 feet, one "door" (or opening) span of 370 feet, one of 110 feet, and will be 40 feet above high water mark ; but its cost will only be £133,000.   The Severn Tunnel is to cost a million, while the bridge over the Mississippi at St. Louis, which is not one third its length, and no wider in one span, cost a million.   It is true that the latter carries a double line of railway and a roadway, still the difference in cost is most striking.

The environs of Cincinnati contain many beautiful villas, amounting almost to country places ; the ground, being broken into hill and valley, affords commanding sites.   The Spring Grove Cemetery, some five miles from the city, 450 acres in extent, is one of the most beautiful burial places I have ever seen, containing many monuments exhibiting high art—one said to have cost £12,000.

The last stage of our long journey may be said to have commenced at Cincinnati, from whence to Washington we have a run of 22 hours, and thence, via Baltimore, to New York, 6 hours.   The Marietta and Cincinnati, and Baltimore and Ohio Railways, between Cincinnati and Washington, traverse the States of Ohio and West Virginia, the latter portion of the route crossing the Alleghany Mountains, in the midst of which I am now writing.

The first 20 or 30 miles of our route lay through a fertile agricultural district, well timbered with hard wood. We then gradually entered a wilder region with a poor yellow soil, and passed along the banks of a small stream with low hills rising about 100 feet on each side, clothed with oak coppice, the strips of flat land in the valley yielding grudgingly, and the scattered cottages of the inhabitants sharing in the poverty-stricken look of the district. The rocks however begin to look like old friends, and soon I see evidences that we have entered on the coal measures again, so that the external poverty may well be compensated by the internal wealth. First we pass an abandoned blast furnace, then the crop of a vein of coal about 4 feet thick, which I trace here and there in the cuttings and hillsides for several miles, dead flat and " in its place " (as we say) with no indication of faulty ground, apparently a very Paradise for the oft-disappointed collier.

At nightfall we approached Parkersburg, on the banks of the Ohio, which is here spanned by a magnificent bridge. The scenery of the Alleghanies has the reputation of being very fine, and we had, therefore, arranged to get our car shunted at Belprè, and then attached to the early morning train. The nights are now cold, and a fine fire blazed in the grate of the comfortable little Inn in which we supped. The coal appeared to me to be of the highest quality for house purposes, a strong binding coal, melting into fine coke, plenty of gas, and very little ash.   It is quite a mistake to suppose that anthracite predominates in America.   On the contrary, the largest coalfields appear to be bituminous, the eastern portion only of this field being anthracite.   At the point where we crossed it is 150 miles wide, and, as I said in a former letter, its length from north to south is about 750 miles.

Its surface characteristics between Parkersburg and its eastern outcrop at the upheaval of the Alleghanies, reminded me very much of Glamorganshire, both as to its configuration and vegetation.   At first valleys of no great depth, like the Llw and Llan ; then larger and deeper valleys, like the Taff, Dare, and Neath, with just such rivers flowing through them, just such steep wooded sides, rising almost into the dignity of mountains, and just such rocky graigs, terminating in rounded outlines.   Pursuing it further, we pass into a country resembling Brecknockshire, Carmarthenshire, Cardiganshire, and so on into the still older formations of North Wales. In fact, a traveller passing north through our coalfield would traverse much the same country outwardly and geologically, as we passed in traversing the Alleghanies from west to east, between Cincinnati and Washington.   The Alleghanies no doubt are somewhat higher, for at one point my aneroid indicated 4,200 feet, but substantially the two districts are very similar.   Fine mountain ranges open out here and there, as one catches glimpses of more distant scenery through the lateral valleys ;

but I can convey no better idea of the Alleghanies to my neighbours in Glamorganshire than by referring them to their own surroundings.

Geologically this railroad section is very interesting, for I could follow the crops of coal veins (and I saw but few) as they rose to the eastern upheaval, until at last we came to a thin bed of Carboniferous Limestone, then to a great development of Old Red Sandstone, then to Silurians, and finally to Gneiss and Eruptive Rocks.

The vegetation, also, is similar to our own. The oak prevails, mixed with beech, birch, maple, and occasional firs. The autumn tints, however, of these forests far exceed in beauty and variety anything I have ever seen. They range from the brightest vermillion to rich purple, brown, and thence to positively transparent gold. No painter dare venture to copy them, for if he did he would be condemned for exaggeration, as well as to inevitable failure. But what interested me almost more than anything else was to discover the rhododendron growing wild in its native woods, forming a large portion of the undergrowth, especially in the bottoms. The coal measure soil, then, is its natural habitat. No wonder it flourishes so luxuriantly in Glamorganshire.

After climbing the steep grades, hugging the sharply-inclined mountain sides, crossing deep ravines on trestle bridges, with clear streams two or three hundred feet below us, we reached the summit level of this Pass over the Alleghany Range, and began to run merrily down the eastern watershed, swinging round the curves in a style which made standing on the rear platform of the car, with one's body disposed to obey the laws of gravitation, and fly off at a tangent, somewhat risky and nervous work. But a training of nine thousand miles had caused the ladies even to be as fearless as French railway guards, and to keep their footing with but little holding on, so that we were able to take in the whole beauty of the Pass as we climbed its western and flew down its eastern sides.

The rivulet below the summit gradually grows into a stream, and the stream begins to assume the dimensions of a river, as we rapidly rush along its banks, and follow its tortuous windings. What is this nascent river? My geography fails me, but the map informs my ignorance. It is a river whose name was often heard in the sad days of the great civil war, now known as the " Recent Difficulty." Its banks were the scenes of many hard-fought battles, its waters were often dyed with fraternal blood. Those who remember those evil days will at once call to mind the " Potomac;" but in charity give it its fine-sounding Indian pronunciation, " Pō-tō-mac."

Just as the shades of evening began to lengthen, we approached a spot striking in its natural features, and ever memorable in the painful annals of that war—" Harper's Ferry," where John Brown was massacred, where an important United States Arsenal formerly stood, where Stonewall Jackson captured a Federal Brigade, and where a hundred other deeds of arms took place. It was a constant centre and focus of strife, and, I was told on good authority, changed hands seventy-six times during the war.

There stand the ruins of the Arsenal (the only ruins caused by the war which I have seen), and there is a shanty close to the railway with the words " John Brown's Fort" painted on it in great white letters. It was there that he was seized before his murder. And yet one would have said that "Harper's Ferry" was one of those lovely spots stamped with the seal of Nature's favour, and worthy of better things than to be made the cockpit of man's evil strife; for the sometime wide valley is here closed in by precipitous cliffs rising perhaps a thousand feet on either side, while a lateral gorge discharges the waters of a not inconsiderable river into the wide Potomac, rushing over its rocky bed.

The triangular spit formed by this junction rises rapidly from the river, and on its curved shoulder one of the most picturesque and old-fashioned looking towns I have seen in America is perched; around, on either side, the cliffs are too precipitous and lofty to admit of defilement by any device of man. If this remarkable spot, instead of being named after the descendant of some evidently nameless bard, possibly possessing a bardic title unpronounceable by the ignorant Sassenach of the fifth century, had received its distinctive appellation by the original " Harper," and had been called " Rhyd Glendwr," or by the Saxon " Teufelsgang," or even by the Yankee

"Hellgate," it would have merited its name and been better known to fame.

But what is that gorge and what is the river which issues from it? That is the south fork of the Shenandoah and its valley — the scene of so many battles that it was popularly known as "the valley of the shadow of death." Tens of thousands of brave men lie buried in that valley who fell in the prime of their manhood, the victims of fratricidal strife. A friend who saw those battle-fields, described them to me as a man might describe some terrible nightmare. But those recollections are rapidly fading away, and the present President appears to be wisely determined to bridge over and heal the remaining breaches, so far as in him lies.

CHAPTER XIV.

WASHINGTON.

PASSING the Potomac on the now restored Trestle Girder Bridge, which, from the narrowness of the gorge, must have presented great engineering difficulties, we sped along the eastern bank, and after the lapse of an hour or two found ourselves approaching the Capital of the United States and driving through its silent streets, over smooth asphalted roads, very different from the usual deeply seamed and pitted thoroughfares of American cities, in passing over which you must be careful not to allow your tongue to protrude lest its end should be lacerated by your teeth.

The very night look of Washington is calmly dignified as befits its mission; its wide avenues scrupulously clean and planted like boulevards; its houses, very varied in character, from the Palace to the old frame shanty, which has been held for a high price; no appearance of civic magnificence or commercial extravagance; here and there a solid and handsome public building gleaming spectrally white in the bright moonlight; the whole endowed with an Athenian sentiment.

The sensation of passing through these dignified silent streets was widely different from that which

C C

I had so often experienced on arriving in the scrambling young giant cities of the west, and the same feeling was confirmed on the morrow, when, under the kind and skilful guidance of our naval attaché, we started to " do " the Capital and Capitol. Unfortunately, the President and Chief Secretaries, as well as our own Minister, were away, and I had no opportunity of making their acquaintance, which I very greatly regret. What would I have given throughout my journey to have been able to multiply my days by three ! ! !

Short of the satisfaction I should have had in making the acquaintance of these distinguished men, our visit to Washington left nothing to desire, and my verdict is that the City and public buildings are worthy of the great people whose national councils are held within them. The Capitol is indeed in all respects well suited to its high functions ; of its kind I can call to mind no statelier pile ; its position is magnificent, standing as it does on the summit of a conical eminence dominating the city, so that great additional effect is given to its massive proportions, which appeared to be architecturally perfect. It is not easy to convey an adequate idea of the Capitol. Many of my readers have been at Paris, and I ask them to imagine the Madeleine, raised on a basement about twice as high as that on which it stands at Paris, and surmounted by a 250 feet dome, flanked by buildings of nearly its own height and in its own style, for some 200 feet on either side, with a row of fine Corinthian columns stretching along their façades, and terminated at either end by buildings greatly resembling the Paris Bourse, with its double rows of columns ; the whole composed of white marble and granite. They will easily understand how imposing such a pile of buildings must be. To those who have been at Rome I would say that the general effect is not very unlike St. Peter's and the Vatican.

The interior is devoted to Congressional uses only : to the Chambers, Committee Rooms, Libraries, &c. ; but no public Departments have their offices within it. They are dissevered from it, both physically and constitutionally, and are grouped around the residence of the President.

We were too late to see the Senate in actual Session, as they had just adjourned, but we spent a couple of hours in the House of Representatives, greatly interested in the proceedings. After an apprenticeship of a quarter of a century, I may be prejudiced in favour of our own forms and rules, but I confess the want of dignity with which the business is conducted in the House of Representatives impressed me most disagreeably. The Chamber is a long, low parallelogram, occupied by a central arena and galleries, with benches or chairs five or six deep around it, and behind them again a wide flat space on which members collect and gossip—an arrangement, as it seems to me, inconsistent with calm and undisturbed deliberation. Indeed, a member informed me that the public occasionally applaud, but that he had never heard signs of dissent or disapproval.

The floor of the House is accessible at numerous points. Opposite to each door a screen is placed, and thus a passage is formed nearly continuously round the floor. In the centre seven rows of chairs and desks are placed in a semicircle, the Speaker, Clerks, and Official Reporters occupying a raised dais in the middle. Gangways at intervals separate the members' seats. The greater part of the Democrats sit on the proper right, while the Republicans occupy the left. The distinction of party seats is not so rigidly adhered to as in our House.

The Speaker has no official dress nor canopied seat. He sits out in the open and springs up with rapid action, bangs his hammer down with alarming vigour, and enters straight into the fray. The grave and stately dignity of our Speaker, rising in the most studiously high-bred manner, and in calm and measured tones, amid absolute silence, giving utterance to dicta never for an instant questioned, forms the greatest possible contrast to what I saw at Washington.

But the practices which appeared to me most subversive of quiet deliberation are the reading, writing, and standing of members in the gangways and on the floor of the house, and more especially the running about of errand boys who lounge near the Speaker's chair, and when summoned by a member clapping his hands, rush to him at top speed. This most unseemly interruption is constantly going on. It is unnecessary to remark how important it is to maintain the strictest order and decorum in a popular assembly, and how much is lost by their absence.

Members of the British Parliament are admitted to the "floor." I was introduced to the Speaker, and subsequently took my seat, almost in the centre, but with a slight list to the Democratic side ; that, however, was accidental, as I took the place of the member who was good enough to introduce me. Luckily, no debate was going on, and I thus had an opportunity of seeing many forms gone through, such as swearing members, presenting Bills, putting the question, taking the voices, counting by rising in their places, challenging the decision, dividing with tellers, and finally, calling over names. They have these four modes of taking divisions, the latter being a very lengthy process. Our system is quick, certain, and open to no cavil.

I by no means approve of their separate chairs and desks. They occupy such a space that I really believe their 270 members take up as much room as our 650, and, as I before said, the inducements thus offered to writing, reading, &c., is most destructive of the attentive debating of any subject. As the number of members increases, so will it become more and more difficult to keep order. The Senate Chamber is similarly arranged.

From the Capitol we drove past the Treasury and other public offices ; they are all of Grecian architecture. The material used in their construction is either granite or white marble, which produces a somewhat wearying sameness. It is therefore not to be regretted that the buildings now in course of erection for the War, Naval, and other departments, are to be in the renaissance style. The residence of the President, called the " White House," is in the Greek or Italian style. I had no means of examining it closely. It stands in its own grounds, and is much like an ordinary first-class English country house ; in fact, I believe it was designed by the same architect who built the Duke of Leincester's house at Carton in Ireland. The British Legation is a creditable building, well suited to its purpose.

We did not omit to visit the cemetery of the soldiers who fell in the civil war and are buried at Arlington, General Lee's old family place in Virginia, and a very touching spectacle it is in more ways than one. We entered the gates of the once beloved home of the great Confederate leader, and drove up a pretty valley with its small stream winding through well-kept grassy glades, terminating in woodlands. On either side of us were rows and rows interminable of small marble stones, eight or ten inches above the ground ; on most of them a simple name, or sometimes none at all, was inscribed.

We reached the summit of the hill on which the old Virginian mansion still stands surrounded by its pretty parterres, summer-houses and vine-clad trelisses, its terrace commanding a splendid view over the Potomac, with the City of Washington and its lofty Capitol to the east. and the reaches of the harbour to the south, a homely and once happy family retreat. No children's toys now occupy its vestibule; it is filled with the relics of the war. No happy laughter now rings through its corridors; all is cold and desolate, and from its windows in all directions are seen long rows of white marble stones with here and there the more elaborate memorial stone erected to the memory of some officer, marking the last resting-places of 11,276 brave men : 7,199 known, and 4,097 unknown, who fell in civil strife, either as foes or under the leadership of the great General, whose childish footsteps once trod those grassy lawns. It was, indeed, a terribly bitter revenge at once to confiscate his patrimony and defile it with dead men's bones ! ! !

An hour's run by rail brought us early next morning to Baltimore, which appeared to me to be so like other American cities that it is needless to describe it ; indeed, time did not permit me to go into any of its details.

From Baltimore sprang two of the leading firms of America, viz., the late Mr. Peabody and Messrs. Brown Brothers, better known in England as Brown, Shipley and Co. Mr. Peabody has richly endowed the City of his early business life. I visited the handsome institution founded by him which will ever remain one of the many enduring proofs of his munificence. I was informed that he began life at Baltimore, really and literally with a pack on his back, travelling the country round to supply the small storekeepers with "dry goods." While others failed, he succeeded by an intimate knowledge of his customers and a keen appreciation of whom to trust and whom not. From that small beginning he became the possessor of a wholesale "dry goods store," and, prudently extending his business in his native country and England, gradually amassed the immense fortune of which he distributed before and after his death so large a portion with such careful munificence.

He always entertained the strongest love for England. I remember meeting him travelling in Italy a year or two before he died, when he told me from whence in England his family originally came,— somewhere in the northern counties, and that he had visited the spot to find out all he could about them. The same feeling on the part of Americans of the third and fourth generation has come under my notice several times, and I believe that a strong love of the Old Country pervades the nation generally.

While at Baltimore I visited a copper works established there, and found it managed by an old White Rock man, and manned chiefly by Welshmen ; it is a small and not very flourishing concern, I fear.

A run of four hours through a flat but fertile and well farmed country, brought us to New York, where three days were spent most agreeably, thanks to the kindness of our friends. The hospitality of Americans exceeds any that I have ever met with, and when the day came for embarking on board the famous old Cunarder "Russia," and we steamed down the magnificent harbour, the sun rising behind

the great City we were leaving, and lighting up its
tall spires and massive buildings till they faded from
our sight as we passed the picturesquely-wooded and
villa-crowned heights of Staten Island on the right
and Long Island on the left, steaming across the bay
and past the famous Sandy Hook Light-house, I
confess that in spite of my face being set homewards,
I could not look back without regret at the country
I was leaving, so replete with all the elements of
future greatness, peopled by a race which no right-
feeling Englishman can regard as other than his
own, and whom I had found so ready to receive me
as an Englishman with the warmest welcome, and
only anxious to manifest in a substantial manner
their appreciation of the close ties which exist between us.   The idea of any serious disagreement
occurring between the two countries appears to me as
monstrous and abhorrent as a blood feud between
members of one family, and I am convinced, that
setting aside professional politicians, the great bulk
of the American people are deeply imbued with the
same feeling.

The Atlantic and the "Russia" are behaving
tolerably, although November is not August.   We
are now rather more than "half seas over" (lat.
46·33, long. 38·52, 1,615 miles from New York and
about 1,500 from Liverpool), and I am bound to confess that for 36 hours the old ship has been in a
most unsteady condition, no wind, and blue mountains rushing down upon us from the northwards,
causing her to roll almost to her gunwale, the cabin

ports at one moment looking into the blue depths and at the next up into the murky sky. Last night, I believe, the good old creature got as far over as she ever gets, and certainly, although I have only about three inches " play " on each side of me in my berth, I found it too wide and had to wedge myself in to prevent gathering way at each roll, while my portmanteau set to work to act battering ram in the dark, until I detected its vagaries and wedged it in also.

I mention these things to show what a winter voyage in these fine steamers is, but at the same time let me say that no one need be deterred from visiting America, for out of 52 passengers 28 of us, including eight ladies, are quite happy, and punctually devour the bountiful and substantial, but rough, shaggy, sea-dog fare set before us. Why our great steamship companies go on loading their tables with masses of joints, geese and turkeys, at no doubt great expense, and do not think it worth while to engage proper cooks, who might not only do the plain cooking well, but also save largely by making entrés out of the unused portions, I cannot understand. The table on board the " Messagerie " and other Foreign Companies' ships is infinitely superior to the Cunard, the Peninsula and Oriental, or any other English Company I know of.

We are now further advanced on our voyage, and only 860 miles from Liverpool. The heavy rolling in a calm was succeeded by a South-wester, before which we have been bowling away grandly, doing our 339 knots in the 24 hours. A "strong breeze" or half-a-gale carried away our main-topgallant sail last night, but all the passengers are on deck and enjoying the fine air and grand sea, rolling in deep blue hills after us, now and then catching us and looking as if it must come on board, but just at the critical moment dying away under the counter and surging forward in a foaming white mass flecked with the loveliest green ; flocks of gulls are hanging close to the wake of the ship, now floating above her on suspended pinion, now swooping round her, now descending as lightly as a snow-flake on the surging sea, and then rising gently over its crests. A fine ship running before a strong breeze in the Atlantic is a sight for the gods. I have been luxuriating in it all day, unable to tear myself away and come down to finish up my notes ere the crush of home work comes upon me.

As I have time on my hands, and little to do on board ship but to read or write, perhaps I may be permitted to close my notes with a few words on the condition of things in general, so far as I have been able to observe them while in America.

And first as to travelling : I had heard that the manners and customs of Americans were rough, and that it was doubtful how far a lady ought to travel in the public railway carriages, or to stay at hotels. I can say positively that a more unfounded idea was never entertained. Both from observations made when travelling for some time in the ordinary carriages, and from what I saw when I passed through the public cars on our long journeys, as well as from frequently using the street cars, I can state that in no country have I ever seen greater politeness shown to ladies, or better breeding generally; even smoking is rigidly forbidden, except in compartments set apart for it, and is never attempted elsewhere. When I contrast this with the disagreeable scenes I have witnessed in regard to smoking in England and Germany, I wonder at our bad manners as much as I admire the American arrangements.

The cars are of three classes—first, second, and third, all with end doors, centre passages, and seats facing one way, and supposed to accommodate two passengers on each side of the gangway. The third class have wooden seats and small windows; the second class cushions; the first class seats have reversible backs, so as to face each other if required; but permission must be obtained from the conductor, and the hinge unlocked, before the back can be changed. These carriages are uncomfortable; the backs are too low, and there is nothing to lean the head against. The arms on one side are generally iron with a little patch of stuffing; on the window side of the carriage all is hard wood with keen edges.

The Pullman cars are of two kinds—"Sleepers," such as I have described at considerable length, and "Drawing-room" cars, which have two or more state-rooms, each holding four arm chairs; the centre of the carriage is provided also with arm chairs on pivots, so that they can be turned in any direction. I travelled one day in such an arm-chair, and found it extremely irksome; it simply did not fit me, and it is evident that an arm-chair must be difficult to construct, so as to be comfortable for a nine-stone lady, five feet high, and an eighteen-stone man, upwards of six feet high; besides which, these chairs lean back so much that at one point the backs touch, and being covered with cotton velvet and brass nails, the back of my chair on one occasion got "into gear" with that of the next lady's chair, and as she fidgetted a good deal, every time she swung her chair a quarter turn round, she swung me equally until we had quite a *dos-à-dos* disagreement.

Upon another occasion I had two babies, of diverse origin, in the Pullman drawing-room car; one screamed for hours, and was at last only quieted by the contents of a suspicious-looking little bottle, after which it slumbered soundly, but whether it ever awoke or slept the everlasting sleep I know not. The other baby had for its guardians a fine Lady Mother, evidently oppressed with the ills of further blessings; a meek Papa of the order which always have quivers full, a quiet patient creature with a longish enduring-looking countenance, straight hair and sparse habit; a smart Aunt, and a rough bouncing Irish girl as nurse, largely developed in every direction—great red cheeks and arms, coarse untidy hair and garments to match. The baby cried, the nurse patted it on the back with a hand fit only to wield a Lifeguard's sabre, and then gave it an orange; it still cried; the Mamma looked at it with upturned lip as if she hated the name of a baby; the smart

Aunt took it for a moment, and failing to pacify it, soon handed it to the meek Papa, who was the only nurse of the lot, and set to work to undo a basket, get out an Etna cooked pap and stuff the brat with it in a business-like way, but alas! to no purpose, for it still "was not happy." No doubt all this was interesting to the parties concerned, but it possessed no special attraction for myself and twenty other people in the car.

Then, again, the question of fresh air or draught is a constant source of divergence of views in these large open cars with ten windows on each side : one individual thinks fresh air the staff of life ; his next neighbour hates a draught, and every breath gives him visions of pleurisy, congestion, ague, fever, and every other ill. Who is to decide between them, and either keep the windows open or shut.

Then in winter, I am told, they heat the cars by stoves and pipes to suffocation point. Under our system none of these evils occur. We avoid babies as we should the plague, and we manage our window as we please. Then, we leave the importunate news-boy behind at Paddington ; but in America he is perpetually circulating through the cars, and teasing you to buy his trash, so that a testy old gentleman is said to have written in large letters and stuck it on his hat, " I want no papers, novels, guidebooks, reviews, cigars, oranges, lollypops, or popcorn."

The state-rooms, I am bound to say, are comfortable, and not open to the objections above enumerated, but one has all the trouble of engaging them beforehand. For day-work give me an English carriage, for night-work a Pullman. All Pullman cars are subject to an extra payment beyond the first-class ticket.

I had also heard that American railways were badly laid and unsafe. No statement can be more erroneous. I travelled between eleven and twelve thousand miles, and on the whole the permanent ways were in excellent order, and as I stood and sat for hours and hours on the rear platform with nothing between me and the rail, I had an excellent opportunity of observing the condition of the roads. Here and there we came upon lengths of old iron rails, and it was not necessary to look at the road to identify them, the shaking and noise were quite enough; but steel has very largely taken the place of iron already, and passengers, no less than shareholders, are enormous gainers thereby. American directors are relaying their lines with steel as rapidly as they can, and at £7 15s. to £8 per ton they can well afford to do so.

The safety with which American railways are worked is very remarkable, especially as they are almost all single lines ; I may say entirely so, except those near the great Eastern cities. The New York central has four lines as far as Albany, and, I believe, further towards Buffalo. The Western lines are all single. This immunity from accident is due to the intelligent use of the telegraph and to rigid rules. I was much struck by the extreme care with which our time schemes were fixed when we were

running "special" or "wild cat" as railway officials
style it.

The speed of American trains is not great except
on the Metropolitan lines between the Eastern cities.
The Pacific lines clear about 20 miles per hour. The
Eastern Expresses about 30. The fares are less than
in England, being from 1d. to 1½d. per mile first class,
against 2d. to 2½d. in England. I think their system of
building carriages may be in some respects better than
ours. The carriage bodies are supported at each end
on "bogies," *i.e.*, platforms, with four or, better, six
wheels, to which they are attached only by a central
pivot; this enables them to go round curves without
grinding against the flanges or straining the sides as
in our rigid system. The Germans have adopted the
American plan, and I believe it to be much safer. On
the other hand our carriages, being only half the
length of American cars, can be made much lighter,
and thus the excessive weight of American trains is
avoided, higher speeds can be attained with less power
and less wear and tear per passenger carried, while the
facility of meeting the demand for places is greater, as
our officials can put on a carriage for 24 passengers,
while the Americans must add a carriage for 40 or
50, perhaps to accommodate a dozen people. The
great strength of American carriages saves life
in accidents, as they do not "telescope." The
American buffers and drawbars are vile inventions.
Now and then you get a shock violent enough to dis-
locate all the vertebræ of your spine. The engines
are on the plan first invented by Mr. Crampton

—two bogie and two coupled driving wheels on each side.

There are no bridges to carry roads over railroads, nothing but level crossings. Where country roads cross they have no gates but dig a deep pit on each side between the sleepers, and fence up to it. No animal will cross the sleepers laid hollow; and if it does stray on to the road the cowcatcher of the engine disposes of it quickly. This cowcatcher, the pneumatic break, and the cord which runs through every American carriage, to sound a gong on the engine, ought to be made compulsory by law in England. In fine, no one need fear to travel on American railroads on account of danger.

CHAPTER XV.

AMERICAN HOTELS.

A FEW words on hotels may not be uninteresting. The hotel is an "Institution" in America. It is often the finest building in the town, and has perhaps cost £200,000 or £300,000. The arrangements of all Hotels are much the same. On entering one generally ascends a flight of steps, designed to give height to the basement, in which the barber's shop, lavatories, laundries, &c., are situated. Having ascended, one finds oneself in a large vestibule or hall; at one side is a long substantial counter, behind which the manager and his clerk stand, and on which a large book lies, in which you enter your name. The blotting paper of this book is printed all over with advertisements; and, on inquiry, you find that the book is supplied gratis by enterprising advertising agents.

At this counter all your business is transacted. Generally there is a notice, "No cheques cashed, or money *loaned*." In one corner of this vestibule is a book and newspaper stall, in another a cigar stall. Passages lead in various directions,—one to the "Bar," where "cock-tails," "mint juleps," "cobblers," "eye-openers," "corpse revivers," and other like beverages, are dispensed. I tried two, and more nauseous mixtures I never tasted. Behind this "Bar" stands an active, clean-looking man, in white apron, shirt-sleeves, &c. ; and around sit and loll the imbibers, who struck me as of the solemn and stupid order, although I had not much chance of judging.

The " office counter " and the " bar " thus replace our snug old English " bar-room," to many, I suppose, the dearest spot of their native town, where the neat barmaid dispenses the substantial old drinks of England with an archness of which the man in the white apron and shirt-sleeves is innocent, for she knows that barmaids have often been elevated to the Peerage, and she has faith in her own fate, until the tooth of time has nibbled away the roses, and then!!—well it has always been a mystery to me, what becomes of ancient barmaids. However, the straight-laced clerk of the office and the shirt-sleeved-cocktail-mixer of American hotels have no such romance about them. Which is best ?

Another passage from the vestibule leads to the writing and reading rooms, another to the reception room and ladies' room, which is also approached by a separate entrance from the street, and generally has a separate staircase near it. Both these are great advantages, because the vestibule is the resort of loafers and loungers, who hang about, and seem to have no fixed occupation except that of prying into other people's concerns. They are a great annoyance to the hotel keepers, but they cannot get rid of them.

F F 2

After registering your name, you are shown to your room, or rather "elevated" to it in the "lift." You find it always clean and well furnished. The good rooms of the best Hotels have private baths and lavatories, with hot and cold water laid on. This is to save labour—a great object in the States—no carrying of water and slops. The beds are good and clean, but there are no tables, except perhaps a small oval marble slab, so that your "special correspondent" has at times had to shift as he could when writing his notes. There are always baths downstairs, generally in the basement, in one of which I saw the following specimen of grammar :—" Gentlemen are requested not to overflow the baths, and oblige the manager !"

In American Hotels, the custom is to board and lodge you at so much per day—from 3 dols. to 5 dols. (12s. to £1)—and I certainly prefer this system to our own of charging each item separately. Wine is extra, but no one drinks it ; in fact, the prices charged for it are prohibitory. The usual price for a bottle of sherry is 2 dols. (8s.) ; champagne, 3 dols. 50c. (14s.) ; claret, 2 dols. (8s.). Breakfast is served from 5.30 to 11 a.m. ; dinner, 1 to 4 p.m. ; supper, 6 to 12. A long list is given, from which you order what you like. I have a ménu before me, consisting of two soups, two fish, five boiled and five roast meats, nine entrés, game, cold meat, and sweets. You are generally kept waiting, however, a long time. The meat is hard and stringy, being kept too long on ice, and the cooking is very inferior. I can only call to mind two Hotels, viz., the Brevoort at New York, and the Grand Hotel at Cincinnati, where things were really well done, and I stayed at the best Hotel everywhere. It would cost no more to have meat well cooked and served, and I can only attribute the badness of the cooking to ignorance of how things ought to be done.

The waiters are generally black men, who are quick and good natured, but run away as soon as they have got their orders, and wait till everything is cooked ; in the meantime no one else at the same table can get anything. The master of the Hotel is generally too great a swell to attend to his guests, or look after the cooking and waiters. I presume no one looks after the cooking, and the waiters are left to their headman.

Many people in America live permanently in Hotels, especially old bachelors, who do not want to be troubled with housekeeping. At Washington, Senators and Representatives are to be found in numbers in all the Hotels, in fact the Hotels appear largely to take the place of lodgings with us. An English watering place is full of lodging houses ; at Saratoga I saw comparatively few, but there were three gigantic Hotels, accommodating upwards of one thousand persons each. I think the American system is better, for it is evident that a large establishment must be conducted more economically than a number of small ones, and that the visitor must have many more luxuries and conveniences than he could have in small lodgings.

Hack carriages, as they are called, are terribly dear. 6s. to 8s. per hour is the common charge, and to a station often 12s. or more for a party of four. You are also charged 1s. for every article of luggage to or from a station sent by the Despatch Company. The American " check " system for luggage is in many respects very good. On going to the " depôt " (*i.e.*, station) you deliver your luggage to the man charged with its receipt, who gives you a small piece of brass with a number on it for each article, and at the same time loops on a corresponding number by a leather thong to the handle of your portmanteau; on arriving at your destination you deliver your checks and claim your luggage, or you leave it at the station and claim it when you want it or send for it. This system does not take longer than pasting on labels, the check itself indicating the destination. There is no weighing or payment for luggage unless it is outrageously in excess of fair passenger wants.

On the whole, travelling is cheaper in America than in England, and it is about the only thing which is cheaper. One might almost say that a dollar represents a shilling, but certainly it would be no exaggeration to say that everything except bread and meat is double as dear in America as in England. This arises chiefly from two causes, the War and consequent depreciation of the currency, and Protection. Gold has now almost reached " par," greenbacks being at only $2\frac{1}{2}$ to 3 per cent. discount, but prices having assumed a high level do not readily

follow the gradual changes of the gold market, especially as the protective tariff prevents foreign competition and maintains a fictitious value generally.

The result is that the whole trade of America is
cramped and paralysed. The high cost of her manufactures makes it impossible for her to compete in
foreign markets with ourselves and Germany, and
she has consequently lost many markets which she
formerly possessed. Her internal power of consumption is diminished, and general stagnation prevails. This is keenly felt in all the commercial
Cities in the East ; and even in Pennsylvania, the
hot-bed of protection, men are beginning to say
" Well, things could not be worse, even if we had
Free Trade."

The interests of the West and South are entirely
in favour of Free Trade. It is one of the burning
questions of the day, second only to the resumption
of specie payments, and no one doubts that before
long a complete Free Trade policy will prevail. A
considerable fall in wages must take place before
America can compete with other nations, but so long
as men are willing, as they now are in America, to
do a good day's work and do it well, the reduction need not be so great, and they will probably
be fully compensated by the cheapening of the
necessaries of life. All articles of clothing, for ex-
ample, at present cost double as much in America
as in England.

Dissatisfaction with the working of their Governments, both National, State, and Municipal, seems

to pervade all ·classes of the community. I have
lost no opportunity of discussing political and social
questions with men of all classes, and I have scarcely
met with one whose feelings did not seem to warrant
the above statement.

I say National, State, and Municipal, because it
must be remembered that the United States are
States united for National or Federal purposes only ;
that the Central Government or Congress deals exclusively with National questions, such as Peace, War,
Foreign Diplomacy, the Army and Navy, National
Taxation, including the Tariff, the National Currency,
and such portions of statecraft as apply to the nation
as a whole, which questions are strictly limited and
defined by the written Constitution ; and further,
that each State has its separate Parliament and
Government, and may enact its own laws, upon any
questions which are not reserved by the written
Constitution for Congressional action.

It was also supposed that by the original Constitution any State might retire from the Union and
become absolutely free.   Perhaps that issue, as much
as Slavery and Protection, was the cause of the Civil
War.   The written Constitution of the United
States can only be altered by a majority of Congress,
with the consent of the President ; then the alteration must be submitted to the Legislative Assembly
of each separate State, and unless it receives the
sanction of two-thirds of the State Legislatures, no
alteration can take place.   But few alterations have
passed through this cumbrous process since the days

of Washington—the abolition of Slavery being the most notable.

To Englishmen, who possess no written Constitution, but govern absolutely through their Parliament, it is difficult to realise this state of things. There can be no question that the Constitution of the United States is far more Conservative than our limited Monarchy; indeed, there are two powers which can and frequently do override the State Legislatures, and even Congress itself, viz., the President and the Supreme Court of Justice, which can and does often declare that an Act is contrary to the Constitution, and therefore null and void; in fact, the Americans have an absolute Monarch and a Star Chamber.

Any Act of a State or Congress dealing with property, such as the Trust Properties of Old Foundations, or with contracts between individuals, if appealed against, may be at once set aside by the Supreme Court. Americans say, " Our property is safer than yours, because it cannot be reached even by Congress, and it is well that it should be so, in view of our Universal Suffrage."

The President is as absolute as the most absolute Monarch. He is elected by a party, and, perhaps, secures his election by the barest majority. The House of Representatives is possibly opposed to his policy, or he may " trim" and throw over the party that elected him. For four years, nevertheless, he is an absolute despot; he can *veto* any Act passed by the two Houses, unless it is passed by a majority

not often easy to obtain.   He dares to do so, because
he is not a Constitutional Sovereign, but notoriously a
party man.   He has no personal object to serve,
because in the vast majority of cases he has no chance
of re-election.   No dynastic considerations influence
him ; because his heir can never hope to succeed
him ; and so he follows the bent of his inclinations,
whatever they may be.

Then, again, the Ministers of State have no seats
in the House of Representatives.   They can introduce no measure directly, and cannot be " in their
place" to explain and defend or modify any proposal
affecting their Department ; neither the War
Minister nor the Secretary of the Navy can introduce and defend his " Estimates," or explain the
necessities of the Service with the management of
which he is charged.   He submits his Estimates in
a printed form, and they are then referred to a Committee, which takes evidence upon them, and recom-
mends such changes as in their discretion they may
deem fitting, thus relieving the Minister of all
responsibility in regard to the administration of his
Department.

This is carrying things too far ; I have often
thought and think still that the passing of " estimates" through our House is one of the broadest
farces played on the stage of public life, and I have
often wished that estimates could be submitted to
the quiet and business-like investigation of a " committee upstairs," but I see how difficult it would be
to do so without divesting the minister of his

responsibility and shifting it on to the committee. Our system, therefore, of referring any special griev- ance to a committee, but allowing the general re- sponsibility to rest on the minister, is, after all, probably the best; at any rate, the American system is fraught with mischief, and I by no means advocate its adoption.

The working of the business of the Houses of Congress may interest some of my readers. It will have been inferred from what I have said above that Committees form an important element in carrying on the business of Congress. The Senate this year has twenty-eight Standing Committees, and the House of Representatives forty-three.

The House of Representatives has Standing Com- mittees on Elections, Ways and Means, Appropria- tions, Banking and Currency, Pacific Railroad Claims, Commerce, Public Lands, Post Office and Post Roads, Columbia, Judiciary, War Claims, Public Expenditure, Private Land Claims, Manu- factures, Agriculture, Indian Affairs, Military Affairs, Militia, Naval Affairs, Foreign Affairs, Territories, Revolutionary Pensions, Invalid Pen- sions, Railways and Canals, Mines and Mining, Education and Labour, Laws, Coinage, Weights and Measures, Patents, Public Buildings and Grounds, Accounts, Mileage, Expenditure of the State, War, Navy, Post Office, Interior, Justice Departments, Public Buildings, Reform of Civil Service, Mississippi Levees, and five Special Com- mittees on special subjects not recurrent.

F F 2

I have given these details to illustrate the working of Congress, and the subjects it takes cognisance of. The Senate has committees on nearly the same subjects. The numbers of members serving on each committee of the Senate is usually nine, and on those of the House of Representatives eleven. There are a few committees of five members, and one of seven.

When Bills are introduced they are read twice *pro forma*, and then referred to the committee appointed to deal with the subject to which the Bill has reference. The committee reports on it either favourably, with or without amendments, or adversely; and it is then debated in the House or Senate. This system is necessitated by the absence of Ministers of State and Government members from the Senate and House of Representatives. Instead of measures emanating from the Government of the day, they are introduced exclusively by private members. No doubt much rubbish might be got rid of summarily and much time saved if we could refer Bills to a standing committee upstairs upon their introduction.

There are seventy-six Senators, two hundred and ninety-one Representatives, and eight Delegates from territories, one from each territory, viz., Arizona, Dakota, Idaho, Montana, New Mexico, Utah, Washington, and Wyoming. The States are thirty-eight in number; each returns two senators.

The number of Representatives depends on population. Thus the State of New York returns thirty-three Representatives, while Nebraska and Nevada return one each. But the influence of each of those small States in the Senate is equal to that of New York. Are there then no anomalies in this bran new representative system ?

Some of my readers may not understand the distinction between a State and a Territory. The former is, as it were, an independent kingdom ; it has a regular representative system within itself, and can enact its own laws on all matters not reserved for the jurisdiction of Congress, while the internal affairs of territories are governed by Congress. Thus Nevada, with some 60,000 inhabitants, is a State, and can govern itself, while its neighbour Utah, separated only by an arbitrary boundary, and containing about three times the population, is still a " Territory " under the tutelage of Congress. But then, if Utah were to be endowed with State rights, it is perfectly well known that bigamy would be at once legalised, and the Americans naturally regard such an eventuality with repugnance. So that Utah will be kept in tutelage until the " Gentile" element gains a clear ascendancy.

The national affairs of the United States are managed by nine Chiefs of Departments, each being subordinate to and under the control of the President, viz., 1st, the Secretary of State, who holds the highest rank in the executive next to the President. His duty is to conduct all correspondence with the Public Ministers and Representatives of Foreign Powers, and generally to manage "foreign affairs.' He is the medium of communication between the President and the several States which go to make

up the " United States." He has the custody of the
great seal, and countersigns all proclamations, com-
missions, and warrants, for pardon and extradition.
He publishes the Laws of Congress, Amendments of
the Constitution, and the admission of New States
into the Union.

Next to him comes the Secretary of the Treasury,
who has charge of the national finances, revenue,
and public accounts, and of the issue of warrants for
money in pursuance of appropriations. He controls
the erection of public buildings, the coinage and
printing of money, the collecting of commercial
statistics, and the lighting and buoying of the coast.
He submits to Congress estimates of the probable
receipts and expenditure for the ensuing year, and
provides for the payment of the public debt. To
carry out all these duties his office is divided into a
number of departments, and he is assisted by a staff
of controllers, commissioners, auditors, treasurers,
registrars, &c. These two departments appear to be
the most important and laborious offices.

Next come the Secretaries of War and of the
Navy: these departments are directly under the
control of the President who is Commander in Chief
of both forces. This appears to be a remarkable
provision for a Republican form of Government, in
view of the struggle of our own country to curtail
the prerogative in regard to a standing army; but
so it is nevertheless.

Then comes the Secretary of the Interior whose
duties are to supervise patents, public lands includ-

ing mines, Indian affairs, education, the census, and other minor matter. As each State really governs itself, the Secretary of the Interior's office becomes of far less importance than that of our Home Secretary.

Next comes the Postmaster General, who also is largely controlled in his appointments, contracts, and the like, by the President.

Next follows the Department of Justices, presided over by the Attorney General, assisted by the Solicitor General. His duty is to give opinions on legel questions arising in the Executive Government, and to superintend the United States Attorneys and Marshals in the States and Territories.

Last comes the Department of Agriculture, presided over by a Commissioner, whose duties are to collect and diffuse useful information on subjects connected with Agriculture, and to acquire and preserve in his office all information he can obtain on that subject by means of books and correspondence, by practical and scientific experiments, and the collection of statistics, also to collect new and valu able seeds and plants, to learn by actual cultivation their value, to propagate those found good and distribute them among agriculturists ; he is assisted by a satistician, entomologist, botanist, chemist, and miscroscopist, and has a propagating garden, seed division, and library. As we have nothing of this kind I have copied his duties at length from the official record, from which indeed, I have epitomised the Executive System of the United States, I hope not at too great length, and not without affording information to my readers.

In spite of the care thus officially bestowed on agriculture, it seemed to me that good farming, in the sense that we understand it, is almost wholly absent in the United States. My only opportunity of judging was from closely observing the state of cultivation as I passed through the various districts by railway. I saw no green crops : I really cannot remember that I saw one turnip or mangold crop in the many thousand miles of country I passed through in September and October. There was also an utter absence of that neatness which distinguishes the well-farmed districts of England : all seemed rough and unkempt. But of course merely passing through a country does not enable anyone to give an opinion of much value upon the condition of its agriculture.

Besides the care bestowed on agriculture by the Central Government, each State has its Annual Show, frequently on a large scale. Much attention is paid to improving the breed of animals. I have no doubt that America will soon possess herds of cattle second to none in England; but I am not so sure as to sheep. I scarcely saw a flock of sheep in the United States, excepting in California, where there were Merino sheep bred for their wool.

The constantly recurring necessity of electing a President is a very serious evil, and one which should make every Englishman value the ancient Constitution under which he enjoys such unbounded freedom of self-government, untainted by any source of excitement and political jobbery. Long before the end of every fourth year the country is convulsed and business interrupted by the approaching election of a President ; no one knows with any certainty what the outcome will be, or how to shape his course safely.

After the President is elected no one knows what his line of action may be. All officers, down to the village Postmaster, may be changed, for party reasons only, and men quite new to the work, and often quite unfit for it, put in. If Americans could only get over the first wrench, and elect a king of the old stock, under the same limited constitutional conditions as our Sovereigns, and weld their separate States into one compact and solid Nation, many of them would be only too thankful.

I cannot help suspecting, also, that they would not be sorry to transform their Senate into a House of Peers. There are fortunes amply large enough to support hereditary rank, and men, who will not now enter political life upon any consideration, would doubtless do their duty as patriotically as our Peers, if not compelled to face the dirt of candidature.

As to aristocratic ideas being foreign to Americans, I do not believe it for a moment ; on the contrary, I believe them to be a highly aristocratic people. Talk of exclusiveness ! Why, an old Bostonian holds his head as high above members of the newer communities as any blue-blooded Norman among us, and so does the descendant of the old Knickerbocker (or ancient Dutch settler) of New York ; into that

G G

privileged circle the outside barbarian can no more
enter than he can gain admission to our most exclusive set, or into the Borghese, Dora, &c., circle at
Rome, or the Quartier St. Germain salons of Paris.
Those who can go back to the " May Flower" are as
proud and exclusive as the direct descendants of
William's Norman knights. And many a Welshman
who reads these lines will, in his heart of hearts, say,
" What are William's Norman knights and Norman
blue-blood ?   Were they not a mongrel cross between
Scandinavian pirates and the ancient Gauls, whose
lands they took and held for only some 400 years
before William's time ?   Did not my ancestors own
the whole of Britain before history began ?   I am
entitled to claim the purest, most ancient, and bluest
blood !   Out with the Normans, the Knickerbockers,
and the ' May Flower.' "   And such is the world, be
it old or new ! !

New York is divided into as many " sets," with as
decided lines of separation, as that of London.   San
Francisco is but thirty years old, and yet its aristo-
cracy is as marked as if it could multiply thirty by
thirty, and go back to the Conquest or Caradoc.

The refinement and luxury of American society is
scarcely exceeded by anything in Europe.   There
are, doubtless, fewer houses of a palatial class in New
York than in London or Paris, but there are large
numbers equal to those of our great squares, and the
richness of their furniture certainly equals if not
exceeds our own.   Fewer servants appear to be
kept, and I saw no really well-turned-out carriages,

with high steppers, bob-wigged coachmen, and 74-inch " Johns," whose merit is measured by their inches, and whose heads are valued only by the powder they can carry. But in ladies' dresses we must yield them the fig leaf, without dispute. I must say that in spite of their hostile tariff and the cruel taxes they have to pay upon their outward adornings, they still will have the cream of creams. A young lady told me that she had once paid 1,600 dollars—£320—duty on one box; and another lady told me at San Francisco that the day before a consignment of dresses had arrived from Paris, and that one dress had immediately sold for 1,200 dollars—£240. There was lace on it, it is true, but so " planned " as to be almost useless for future wear. Every American lady of fashion has her measure in the books of Mr. Worth, Laferriere, or some other Paris dressmaker, and many cross the Atlantic for no other purpose than to bring home a fresh outfit and cut down their rivals. An American lady thinks no more of such a voyage than our ladies do of running over to Paris for Easter.

This was not always so, and you may see the steady old Quaker parents, the old lady in her poke bonnet, russet brown gown and neat white shawl; the gentleman in his snuff-coloured cutaway, knee breeches, gaiters and shoes, half scandalised, half proud of the dashing daughter in gorgeous array trailing her yards of satin, much as a hen who has all unconsciously brooded over the eggs of a duck, watches her bantlings when, like the pretty little Quakeress, they obey their natural instincts, and plume themselves on the turbid waters of this troublesome world.

The fashionable and the great of America are the same as their like among us; their manners are as polished, their refinement quite as great, but there is a kindliness and heartiness about them which is usually wanting in our great world, and to meet which, with us, you must go to the country home of your friend.

In this respect I believe that Americans have by no means come up to our standard. The idea of possessing great landed estates and making them their homes during at least half the year, has not entered deeply into the American mind. They have no domains upon which their ancestors have been seated for hundreds of years. They have Villa life on the banks of the Hudson or some other favoured spot, but country life amidst broad acres is unknown to them. Their land is split up into small holdings of 100 to 200 acres, and universal pot hunting has improved all game off its face. You must go far afield to get your gun hot in America. I doubt much whether a country is the better for its young men hanging about cities and threading balls through croquet hoops rather than breasting the hill or charging the ox fence in the grand excitement of a run with a fast pack across a stiff country.

There is nothing an American is more anxious to become acquainted with than our country house life; perhaps a time may come when those who realise large fortunes may desire to invest them in land; at present the Americans appear to have no such instincts. The man of millions may be seen any and every day sitting by his window in the Fifth Avenue labouring at fresh railway combinations to pile up more useless millions. Our views of happiness are different, and our early habits have much influence on them. Perhaps the proprietor of the *New York Herald* is not so happy in the Belvoir Country, where he is now hunting, as Mr. Vanderbilt in his window in Fifth Avenue, where he is probably now sitting. The custom of dividing fortunes among children equally has much to do with the disinclination of wealthy Americans to acquire large landed estates.

CHAPTER XVI.

" REPUBLICAN " AND " DEMOCRAT."

As to the political parties which divide America
—" Republican" and " Democrat"—I can only say
that, having done my best, I have failed to arrive at
any broad line of distinction. No doubt the Republicans were the anti-slavery party; but that is all
over. The resumption of specie payments is a Democratic ticket, but gold is now only at $2\frac{3}{4}$ per
cent. premium, so that it is no longer a burning
question. The double standard of gold and silver is
an open, but only a momentarily exciting topic; it
will be adopted, but for reasons which probably will
never be published, and do not appear in the report
of the committee on that question.

Free Trade and Protection is a burning question.
The Democrats in the main are for Free Trade, but
they are rather fearful to approach it too closely, or
to pledge themselves too deeply; while the Republicans have been afraid to oppose it too vigorously,
the fact being that they are both fighting for Party
and not Patriotic motives. Nevertheless, come
from which side it may, Protection is doomed to
a very short existence in America, and it is well
for the country that it is so. I hear that in the
Universities even, a large proportion of the students

are Free Traders : but the question will not wait for their maturity.

I am not prepared to say that England is likely to be greatly benefited by Free Trade with America. I believe that she can produce every article as cheaply or cheaper than we can, if she will only cease to interfere with Nature's laws and allow the general value of her products to find their natural level. Wages must fall, but the cost of living must fall also ; America will then be able to compete with us in foreign markets, and a most formidable competitor she will be. That we shall ever hereafter be able to compete with American manufacturers in their own home markets, I greatly doubt.

It will be understood from what I have said that such matters as Education, Poor-relief and the like, are State and not National Questions, and as the practice is different in each of the 38 States, it is not unnatural that any one who desires to obtain a comprehensive idea of a country so vast as America, and has only 100 days to do it in, should be unable to go into the details of the administration of so many different States. I must, therefore, simply say that few States, I believe, have regular Poor Laws, although there are many charitable institutions, and in some I saw regular workhouses.

On the other hand, in the matter of Education, I believe no State has failed to organise a most complete system, by which instruction is provided *gratis* for all ages of children from five years old and upwards, ending only with and including the High

Schools and Colleges. The cost is met by rates levied on the real and personal property of the district within which the schools are situated. In this respect America is many years in advance of England, and the system of education is still far more complete.

I was much struck in travelling through the country by the size of the school buildings as compared with the apparent extent of the town or village, and the class of houses of which it was composed. In America almost all houses in the agricultural districts are "frame houses," *i.e.*, wooden frame work boarded over; but the School House is generally a substantial stone fabric. In the most out-of-the-way places on our road to the Yosemite Valley we passed school houses without apparently any habitations near them : the children ride and drive miles to attend them.

The nature of the instruction may be gathered from the following short extracts from the syllabus of the Cincinnati Schools, which I believe may be taken as fairly representative, embracing the twelve years of school life :—1st year—Slate-work, Penmanship, and Drawing. 2nd year—The same, with Mental Arithmetic, Grammar, and Spelling. 3rd—The same, plus German, Composition, and Written Arithmetic. 4th—All the foregoing, plus Geography and Music. 5th—The same. Then come what are called " Intermediate Schools." 6th year—All the above, plus the Rules and Principles of Arithmetic. 7th—The same. 8th—The same ; but from the list

of text books I have before me, and the examination
papers, it is easy to see, although it would be too
tedious to specify, the advance made in each year.

Then come the High Schools. 9th year—Latin,
History, Algebra, and German. In the 10th year—
Physiology, Physical Geography, French, and Greek,
are added. 11th year—Geometry, German, Natural
Philosophy, English Literature, Botany, French, and
Greek. 12th year—Greek, Latin, French, Survey-
ing, Chemistry, Mental Philosophy, Geology, Natural
History, English Literature, and Book-keeping.
Many of these subjects are of course optional, and
most children do not complete the course; but edu-
cation of the above class is open to all without payment, and at their own doors.

Imagine the immense advantage which such a system of general systematic education confers on the
community. Think of the poor widow left with a
large family, and the burden of their education upon
her as well as that of finding their daily bread—how
eagerly does she strive in England to get her boys
into the Blue Coat School and her girls into Howells'
Charity or some kindred institutions; how hard and
often how hopeless are her efforts. Think of strug-
gling professional men or clergymen, and the difficulties they have to encounter. They know well
what education means, and they eagerly desire to do
their duty by their children by conferring its benefits
upon them. I fear they are often compelled to deny
themselves, some even of the necessaries of life, in
order to keep their boys at school. We have met the

H H

case of working men by our Board Schools, but what have we done for those whose struggles in life are often harder ? We shall never be able to call our system of education "National" until it embraces the teaching required by all classes without payment of any kind, the cost being met by a general rate, as in America, and the rate need not be a large one. In some cases portions of land have been set apart to provide funds for educational requirements, and thus local rates are relieved. In the main, however, the expenses are borne by the ratepayers.

Before I leave the question of education, I desire to say that while I admire the completeness of the American system as a national and local institution, I in no way desire to see our great public school system interfered with. I believe that system turns out better men than any other in the world.

While thus caring for the mental culture of the young, the State and municipal authorities are not unmindful of the bodily health and enjoyment of their citizens. I have in the course of these notes occasionally alluded to the Parks which have been created near the large cities which I visited. I believe that I shall not overstate the case if I say that every town of any size has now its Park, provided and maintained by the local authority, for the free use of the inhabitants, and that with no niggardly hand or misplaced economy. The Park at New York is 800 acres in extent ; that of Philadelphia is more than double as large. Chicago has, I think, three Parks, each of considerable size. The one which runs along the shores of Lake Michigan was almost created by depositing the debris of the great fire on the low land adjoining the Lake. San Francisco has won its Park from the arid desert and sandy dunes of the Pacific shore. I might go on describing my drives through the Parks of the various cities I visited until both my readers and my pen were weary.

The moral I wish to draw is, that the American local authorities are far-seeing enough to appreciate the advantages which accrue to the communities they preside over from the retention of spaces for public purposes, where their citizens can breathe untainted air, where the child can make its daisy chain on the green grass instead of its mud pie in the pestilential gutter, where the young can develop their muscles in manly games instead of undermining their health and imbibing bodily and mental poison in the music hall or billiard saloon, where the tradesman can, after harnessing his business nag to his light waggonette, trot out his wife and family for a wholesome airing instead of boosing in some bar room.

The lawns are well kept, and I saw hundreds of men and lads playing on them, some at "base ball," a species of "rounders," of which they are extremely fond all through the States and Canada ; some at cricket, some at croquet. At Philadelphia I saw six full-grown niggers, dressed in black coats and white waistcoats, gravely playing croquet in the Park.

The walks are well kept, and are thronged by
those who cannot afford carriages. The roads are
excellent, the only good roads I saw in America,
and are crowded with vehicles of all kinds. They
generally manage to have a piece of water, on which
the "aquatics" disport themselves; in fact, the
Americans thoroughly enjoy their Parks, which have
now become institutions among them.

This was not always so, for I found that most of
the Parks are of comparatively recent creation.
There has been a great awakening to their necessity
in America. Why not in England? Local taxes are
as burthensome in America as with us, and yet they
tax themselves to provide Parks.

The State authorities are so fully aware of the
advantage of free spaces that they have passed Acts
devoting the most striking and beautiful creations of
Nature within their dominions to the use of the
public for ever. The region of the great trees of
California and the Yosemite Valley have been set
aside by Act of Congress as public property; so in
the same way the singularly beautiful spots in the
Rocky Mountains, near Denver, now called the
"North," "Middle," and "South" Parks, have been
reserved for the use of the public, and cannot be
occupied by settlers.

These so-called Parks are plains covered with
luxuriant vegetation and occasional groves of fine
timber trees, walled in by the loftiest ranges of the
Rocky Mountains, and watered by the purest
streams. Their area is great; that of the North

Park, I believe, I before stated to be somewhat
larger than the whole county of Glamorgan, about 70
miles long and 30 wide. Through these lovely wilds
now roam the bear, the antelope, and the wapiti
(here called elk) in considerable numbers; but unless the authorities interfere to protect them, the
ruthless pot hunter will soon as completely clear
them out as he has done in the older settlements of America. It is a pity that the Governments of the _ United States and Canada cannot
combine to prevent further desecration of Nature's
grandest work, "Niagara." Thus it is abundantly
evident that the necessity for open spaces has
taken deep root in the American mind. May it
do so in our own.

We are no doubt many of us heavily taxed and
many of us may feel that much unwisdom has prevailed in our local expenditure. To my mind it has
for some time seemed that no greater folly was
ever committed by a civilized nation than our expenditure on sewers. I look upon it that we have
by their construction created a huge manufactory of
pestilential gas beneath our feet which, in spite of
" traps " and hydraulic contrivances, will prepetually
and insiduously issue forth, carrying its deadly poison
into the palace of the prince and the crowded alley,
with like deadly effect. Human ingenuity or
insanity could invent no better method of breeding
malarious poison than by pouring out all the refuse
of our houses into sewers with abundance of atmos-
pheric air to aid its decomposition, and by at the

same time giving great facility for the reintroduction of the poison, in a gaseous form, through every ill-made joint and rat-hole in the connecting drains.

And all the while, to carry out this precious system, we waste millions and millions worth of those fertilising agents which, in the economy of nature, were provided for perpetually maintaining the fertility of our soil.

If we devised means of properly economising these fertilising agents which we now spend our millions in wasting, it is scarcely an exaggeration to say that we should have little need to send so many millions across the ocean to buy our food, nor need we seek for and utilise, as one of our most valuable fertilisers, the excreta of saurians which disported themselves on the mud of the Cam unknown centuries before the creation of man.

Nature has placed the means to effect this great economy within our reach in the simplest form ; she has endowed all soils with marvellous powers of neutralising noxious matters, and at the same time retaining their fertilising properties. A day must come when the well known system of availing ourselves of this most valuable property with which common earth has been endowed will be generally adopted, and when our costly sewers will be conduits for rain water alone; then they will breed no more typhoid and other evil consequences of malarious gas, then nothing but the debts, sad mementos of the folly and ignorance of this our generation, will remain to our descendants to pay and bewail.

I have frequently alluded to the number and costly character of the Churches in America, and perhaps I ought to say a very few words on the religous position in that country. I have no more statistics than I have given from time to time. I cannot say how many of the 40 millions of Americans are ranged under one or other of the denominations into which the Christian Church is divided; nor from my point of view would it be a matter of any importance to be acquainted with such statistics. I can draw no distinction between the great Christian sects of America which, with trifling differences, more of discipline than doctrine, are travelling side by side along the same road, and with the same high mission in view.

There is no Established Church, of course, nor could I see or hear that its absence was felt. There appeared to be ample accommodation for religious worship everywhere; not alone in the great cities, but in the country villages in which as we passed along, I always saw one or more Churches. The buildings were substantial and frequently costly. The outward adornment of Churches appeared to be the aim of all denominations alike. The old wish for simplicity in Church architecture seems to have passed away entirely.

I suspect that denominationalism is not half so strong a sentiment in America as it is with us. I was much struck at New York with the replies my friends made to my question, "What Church is that?" The reply generally was, "That is Mr. So and So's Church." "But what denomination?" "Well, let me see, I think he is such and such." It seemed to me that "Mr. So and So" was the stronger element of the two—that the "personal" outweighed the "denominational."

At the time of the rebellion, 100 years ago, the Episcopal Church sided with the Royal Party and incurred great odium. Three generations have scarcely sufficed to obliterate that feeling; but now, I am told, she is receiving great accessions, and I rather fancy it is more "fashionable" to belong to the "Old Church" than to any other sect. Ritualism is rearing its head, but there is a great preponderance of feeling against it. The Sabbath is marvellously well observed—almost more rigorously than in England; all shops are closed and work suspended.

I must not omit in thus summarising the chief features of American life, to allude to the only feature which can be permanently connected with death, viz., the sacred spots set apart for the resting-place of all that remains of poor mortals when once the breath of life has passed from its frail tenement. Nothing can exceed the beauty of American cemeteries. They are generally one of the points of interest to which a stranger is conducted, and except for their melancholy character, they are well worthy of his notice.

In most cases a secluded site is selected, the surface being of varied and irregular contour. Roads and paths follow the undulations and depressions with constant windings, so that no stronger contrast can be conceived than the cities of the living and the dead. The one is made up of nothing but straight lines and angles; the other has every winding and curve to be found in the works of Newton or our Lord Lieutenant. The line of beauty lies with the dead.

A large staff of men must be employed; for no pleasure ground I have ever seen is kept in more perfect order, while the monuments are costly, and in good taste for the most part. Some are very touching and suggestive. So far as I know, the cemeteries of England are far inferior to those of America, excepting always our old village church-yards, the yews in some of which I believe are older than the Christian Era, and point to God's Acre, having been "The Grove" of an earlier worship.

CHAPTER XVII.

MINERAL RESOURCES.

I DO not know that I can say much more on the mineral resources of America than I have said incidentally when passing through the various mining districts, but perhaps a few general remarks may not be without interest.

So far as I was able to judge, America possesses every principal mineral, except tin, in great abundance. Her coal fields are gigantic. The quality appeared to me to be excellent, and the price at which it is sold to the Pittsburg Works proves that it is cheaply got. There are, in fact, few parts of England where coal of like quality can be produced at this moment at so cheap a rate. The cost and quality of coal is the basis of almost every manufacturing industry, and I cannot see, therefore, what is to prevent America from becoming, not only entirely self-supplying in all branches of manufacture, but also a largely exporting country, if only frail man will leave nature's laws to have their free sway.

America possesses iron ores of the finest steel-making qualities and in vast abundance. That she will ever again depend on England for iron or steel seems to me impossible. She is beating us in hardware. I took some pains to go over the stock of an intelligent ironmonger in Canada, and in many articles he proved to me the superiority of those of American manufacture—saws, locks, joiners' tools, and the like.

We all know the extraordinary ingenuity of various American machines for saving labour. Our ladies owe the sewing and our agriculturists the reaping machine, with countless other clever mechanical contrivances, to American inventors. I was told that by their automatic machinery they are even beating the cheap labour of Switzerland in the manufacture of watches and clocks.

If our iron, steel, and mechanical industries are to hold their own, every man from the master to the mechanic, from the capitalist to the handworker, must exert himself and all the intelligence that God has given him to the full. There must be no scamping of work, or restricting of the due hours of labour, nor must there be disagreement and cross purposes : all must pull cordially together or we shall be left behind in the race.

America seems to possess all other of the important metals in equal abundance, with coal and iron. The region of Lake Superior supplies her with some twenty-two thousand tons of copper annually of the very finest quality that I am acquainted with; so much so, that American brass makers by the aid of the high quality of this copper and that of New Jersey spelter, have been able to meet the specifications of the Russian and Turkish Governments for cartridges, punched out of the solid in such a fashion as no brass made from ordinary copper and spelter would stand, and thus the Americans have had the largest share of the supply of cartridges for the war which is now raging.   Time was, and I remember it well, when the United States drew the bulk of its supplies of copper and spelter from this country. Besides the great district of Lake Superior, copper is found in Vermont and in various other localties along the eastern coasts of America.   It is also found in the States of Colorado and California, though in no great abundance.

I have alluded to the great lead production of Missouri and the districts centering at St. Louis, through which market alone 24,000 tons of lead annually pass.   Utah and California are already large lead-producing districts, and are being rapidly developed, yet but a few years ago the United States drew its supplies of lead from England.

I need scarcely allude to the gold and silver production of California, Nevada, Utah, and Colorado. The production of silver in the United States, which in 1868 was only £2,400,000, was estimated to have been £7,000,000 in 1875 ; the whole production of the world being about £14,000,000.   The production of the United States in gold may be taken at about £8,000,000 annually, while that of the world is estimated at from £17,000,000 to £18,000,000. These figures will show that the United States now produce nearly one-half the precious metals of the world, while but a few years ago they produced none.

Quicksilver, which plays so important a part in the metallurgy of gold and silver, is at hand in the heart of the Pacific Mining Districts,—as if Providence had ordained that nothing should be wanting to their prosperity. In 1874 California produced 27,000 flasks of $76\frac{1}{2}$lbs., worth about 6s. per lb., say £43 per flask, say £600,000. But for the fortunate existence of quicksilver in their midst, the mines of California and Nevada would have had to pay an exorbitant price, for in former days it was the monopoly of one great firm. Now California supplies her own wants, and exports two-fifths of her production.

When we reflect that thirty years ago scarcely one of the minerals to which I have alluded was produced at all, and that at this moment each one, in its respective class, excepting coal and iron, probably nearly equals any other similar production in the world ; and that in this short period the United States has passed from an importing to an exporting country, it is difficult to foresee to what extent her mineral wealth may develope itself in time to come, especially when we consider the vast areas over which, in all geological probability, these mineral deposits extend.

I have said that the areas of the American coalfields are enormous. They are stated in the Report of our Royal Commission on Coal, at page 249 of the second volume, at 220,166 square miles, of which only 4,800 are anthracite. I have caused the areas shown on my geological map (which, although official, is on too small a scale to insure complete accuracy) to be measured, and it comes out 251,123 square miles of true coal measures. In addition to these areas, it was supposed in 1871 that there were 200,000 square miles of lignites, tertiary, and other inferior coal adjoining the Rocky Mountains. The samples I saw of this latter coal enable me to say that it is valuable fuel. When we compare these stupendous areas with those of the United Kingdom, amounting to only 2,920 square miles (that of South Wales alone being 906 square miles), and yet consider that our Commission arrived at the conclusion that we have more than ninety thousand millions of tons yet unwrought, the probable amount of coal in America will appear too vast for the human mind to grasp,—as impossible to realise as the distance to the nearest fixed star or the countless hosts of heaven. I assume always that the coal section of these areas is about equal to our own, which I believe it to be. Truly if the world is to last till the coal of America is exhausted, its end must be very remote.

Its prospective metallic resources seem equally boundless, taking a general and theoretical view of them, based on the occurrence of the various geological formations and their proved productiveness so far as developed. Along the eastern coasts of America there is a band of Eozoic and Silurian rocks, some 200 miles wide, extending from the far north nearly to the Gulf of Mexico, in which considerable deposits of copper are found, beginning with the great deposits of copper ore at Betts' Cove in Newfoundland. These rocks, where I saw them, seemed to me to be almost identical with those of Cornwall.

Along the whole of the north of America the same rocks prevail until they are lost beneath the cretaceous formations about the 96th parallel of west longitude, to appear again however in the same line about 12 degrees further west, and thence to extend to the Pacific. In this last mentioned range, the great Lake Superior Copper Mines occur. In the centre of America, between the coal fields, the Silurian, Devonian and Lower Carboniferous rocks, which produce the great lead deposits of Missouri, occupy the entire area up to 95 degrees west longitude; from thence to the Rocky Mountains, at the 105th parallel, we have Coal measure, Cretaceous and Tertiary formation, and then begin the enormous gold and silver bearing formations of the Rocky Mountains and the Sierra Nevada, about a thousand miles wide and twelve hundred long, from the British Possessions in the North to Mexico in the South.

In this great area patches of Cretaceous and Tertiary rocks occur, but in the main it is one great mass of Eozoic and Igneous Rocks, which, wherever they have been prospected, appear to contain veins of the precious metals of greater or less richness. Thirty years ago none but the trapper had set his foot within these wilds, and now they are producing half the gold and silver of the world, and that from a band of country chiefly dependant on the Pacific Railway, which has opened a means of access.

So far as I can see, no special geological conditions exist on that line. Lateral narrow guage railways have been run out for a certain distance it is true on each side of the Pacific line, and rich districts have thus been opened up, but I cannot help believing that as these railways are extended, and as other east and west lines of communication are pushed through this wide region of mountains, far to the north and south of the present Pacific line, fresh mineral districts will be opened up and the present production of bullion increased, or at least maintained. Time and toil alone can realise my forecast.

I can call to mind no subject of general interest upon which I am competent to write which I have omitted in my rough and hasty sketch of the condition of things in America, but before I close my notes I must devote a few lines to Canada, a subject which ought to command our deepest interest. It ill becomes Englishmen to undervalue Canada. We are perhaps too apt to think of it as a Hyperborean region inhabited by a mixed, and largely by an alien race, which sends us timber of the nature of papier maché, and gives us occasionally some trouble and anxiety.

My opportunities of observation in Canada were slight, and I speak with all diffidence; but I am bound to say that although my feelings on entering Canada were somewhat akin to those I have described, I left her with a very different estimate of her worth. I had absolutely no opportunity of

judging of the French-speaking population, but I
was told that they are more than contented with
their government, and thoroughly loyal to their
Sovereign. Quebec, their ancient capital, with its
quiet grass-grown streets and faded grandeur, is
perhaps a visible symbol of the old French communities ; Montreal, of the bustling vigorous
Anglo-Saxon life, which is pushing Canada forward
in the world's race—commerce is thriving there
and in some other of the young towns of Canada.

Nature has not endowed Canada with coal fields
excepting only those of Nova Scotia and New
Brunswick, which are too remote to benefit the
interior, however important in themselves and to
their own district. The chief export of Canada
is timber, and that must in process of time cease.
Metallic mines will probably be developed, for the
geological formations of which she consists are
identical with those of the United States, which
prove so productive on the southern shores of Lake
Superior.

The area embraced in the Dominion of Canada to
the North is as large as that of the United States
themselves, and much of it in process of time will
doubtless be inhabited. The climate is severe in
winter, but probably not more so than in much of
Northern Europe. In summer the weather is delicious, crops ripen rapidly, and in the portions of
Canada between Lakes Huron and Ontario some
of the finest land and the best farming in North
America are to be found. I believe, in fact, that

K K

Canada must look to agriculture for her future development, and probably chiefly to her North Western possessions, so recently visited and graphically described by her Governor-General, who has won the hearts of Canadians so completely that the task of his successor will be no easy one.

Grave responsibility rests on those who are called upon to select a Governor-General for Canada, and they cannot do better than take Lord Dufferin as their model. The Canadians are loyal to the backbone—more English than Englishmen; but they are sensitive and proud of their country, and unpleasantness might easily arise from the injudicious acts of a Governor-General.

They value their freedom far too much to entertain the slightest wish to be incorporated with the United States. I believe if the dominion were polled, not one man in fifty would vote for annexation. Indeed, as I told a bumptious American, who said, "Oh, we shall soon annex Canada," "There is much more chance of Canada annexing you than of your annexing Canada, for the simple reason that you are all discontented with your system of government, and would be only thankful to possess the same as Canada, while Canada is thoroughly contented and happy under her form of government."

There is one bad feature in the present condition of public feeling in Canada. Under the hostile tariff of the United States, Canadian opinion is drifting rapidly towards protection. I hope that ere they take such a fatal step as to enact protective duties, the States will have struck off the shackles which fetter their commerce, and that Canada may be saved from herself.

And now my notes have ended. Weeks have slipped away since I looked through the thick glass of my " port " in the good ship " Russia," about four o'clock on the dark morning of the 16th November, and saw the Fastenet Light (Cape Clear) dancing over the troubled waters, since, four hours afterwards, I stood on the well-known deck and saw the Cove of Cork crowded with shipping—driven in by stress of weather, gradually open as we glided on, since the pilot gig boarded us and the tug ranged up alongside with letters and newspapers only one day old. It was a lovely calm morning, just breeze enough to fill the sails of a splendid American full-rigged ship which came spanking after us with every sail set to her royals. The inclosures of untidy Ireland looked neatness itself after American farming as I swept them with my glasses, and there were the country houses, the luxurious homes of England, nestling among woods, with well-kept lawns running down to the water's edge.

Then followed the calm and pleasant run up channel, so different from its rough behaviour on our outward voyage; plenty of shipping, a relief after a whole week without sighting a sail, which much surprised me, for I thought in my ignorance that the Atlantic was nearly as much thronged as the Straits of Dover; and in the distance the blue

outlines of the Wicklow mountains were just visible.
Then nightfall, and light combining with light to
point us on our way.   Then the last night on board,
and the hubbub on deck, as in the murky glimmering
of a Mersey November morning the tender came
alongside, and strange faces boarded us; and then
the ills of life began—care of luggage, hustle of
landing, and the like.

But one's foot is again on the firm soil of Old
England, and we are soon flitting through the
pleasant pastures of Cheshire.   How neat it all
looks after the snake fences and weed grown lands
of America.   And then we leave the civilised districts and run through the valleys of dear old
Wales, with mountains of very respectable dimensions towering over us.   The names of the stations
have a homely sound, and the tongue of the
Cymri is once more heard, and then we rush
through the well-known wood where many a good
day's sport has given us fresh vigour, and many a
cock has flown his last flight, and then we emerge
into the fine bay, with its triune headland and
sweeping outlines, and then—well, then we are very
soon in our "bright and happy homes," with hearts
ever thankful for the health and safety vouchsafed
to us during our long journey of nearly seventeen
thousand miles.

THE END.

PRINTED AT "THE CAMBRIAN" OFFICE, WIND-STREET, SWANSEA.

www.ingramcontent.com/pod-product-compliance
Lightning Source LLC
Chambersburg PA
CBHW020349030726

47496CB00007B/2062